King's (*The Traveling Man*, 2015) latest thriller picks up the trail of his married con artists as they descend on a software company. . . . After surviving their previous con in Seanboro, this ruthless, manipulative couple once again hopes to fleece a deserving mark. . . . Personal lives, however, tend to skew even the best-laid scams. . . . King returns in fine form with his devious creations in tow. . . . The violence here, though brief, is unexpected . . . the repercussions electrify the narrative. . . . King strikes another vein of modern noir gold. . . ." — *Kirkus Reviews*

Theft. Deception. Murder. The Travelers, husband and wife con artists going by the names Joe and Tess Campbell, agree to wreck a computer server and steal a newly developed data-mining program. A simple, lucrative job. Or it would have been if their employer had told them half the truth. Instead, they discover that they've been thrown into a poorly-planned, amateur scam that turns into a maze of deception and betrayal. Nothing is as it seems, and the Travelers must scramble if they are to stay ahead of both the criminals and the police. The Computer Heist is a fast-paced crime thriller that keeps you guessing until the very end.

The Travelers
The Traveling Man: Book One
The Computer Heist: Book Two

The Computer Heist

The Travelers: Book Two

Michael P. King

Blurred Lines Press

Blurred Lines Press
The Computer Heist
Michael P. King
ISBN 978-0-9861796-4-8

Cover design by Paramita Bhattacharjee at
creativeparamita.com

The Computer Heist is a work of fiction. The names, characters, places, and events are products of the author's imagination.

For Sarah, only and always her.

1: The Negotiation

On a cold Wednesday afternoon in February, the Traveling Man and his wife, currently going by the names Joe and Tess Campbell, sat on one side of a well-worn green vinyl booth in the back corner of a Perkins restaurant opposite Samantha Bartel, who had contacted them about a possible job. They were all eating pie and drinking coffee, each side sizing up the other, trying to decide how to develop enough trust to begin talking about the details. Joe Campbell was fifty-three, just over six feet, pudgy around the middle, with salt-and-pepper hair, a black mustache, and a nose broken slightly to the right. He had a face that was hard to remember. He wore a blue suit, a white shirt without a necktie, and a simple gold wedding band. His wife, Tess, was forty-four years old, though she looked thirty-nine. She was blonde with brown eyes, all curves on a dancer's frame. Even though her shoulder-length hair was pulled back in a bun and she wore a conservative blue suit with a single strand of pearls, she exuded an infectious sex appeal.

Joe ate a forkful of blueberry pie and washed it down with coffee. He glanced out the window at the cars in the near-side parking lot, searching for anyone who looked like a cop, but all the cars were empty. "So Samantha — it's okay that I call you Samantha?"

She nodded.

"How do you know Marky?"

Samantha looked at him carefully. She hadn't taken off her charcoal overcoat. She sat hunched down in it, looking even smaller than usual, and held her coffee cup with both hands.

Her dark hair, cut short, was laced with gray. She had the start of a double chin. She wore no makeup or jewelry. She was plump, apple-shaped, and the tailored gray suit she wore made her look fat. "He used to work for me a long time ago."

Joe rubbed his chin. He didn't like her evasiveness. "As a civilian? That would be a really long time ago."

"Yeah, before he and his girlfriend hacked into the IRS database."

"Ten years in federal prison. And he said I might be able to help you."

Samantha pushed her fork around in the chocolate pie filling still left on her plate. "He said you were the guy to see."

Joe rubbed his hands together as if they were cold and then, prayer-like, tapped his fingers against his chin. He and Tess hadn't committed to anything. They could still get up and walk away. "So he told you how to get in touch with us."

"That's right."

"How did you find Marky?"

"He used me as a reference to get a job."

Joe smiled. "And you helped him out?"

"Sure. He's a talented guy. A good worker."

Joe glanced at Tess. She was stirring sugar into her coffee. "What did Marky say that we do?"

"He said you could" — she looked around and then lowered her voice — "collect materials that others weren't able to collect without drawing attention to yourselves."

Tess chuckled. "That's an interesting way of putting it."

Joe watched Samantha's eyes. "Let me apologize in advance if this seems indelicate, but I want you to go in the ladies room with Tess and prove you're not wearing a wire."

Samantha blinked, clenched her teeth, and shrugged out of her overcoat. Her face colored pink. "Okay." She started to get up.

Joe and Tess exchanged a glance. Tess reached across and patted Samantha's hand. "You're okay. Sit down."

Joe pushed back in his seat to keep a better eye on two men wearing jeans, insulated work coats, and ball caps who were sitting four tables away. "You think you're in our price range?"

"I don't have any idea."

"We start at one hundred thousand plus expenses. Fifty thousand up front. Or half the action, assuming that it's more than a hundred thousand plus expenses."

"That's a lot of money."

"We offer a lot of value."

"I'll give you twenty-five thousand up front."

"We have to hear the job, but if it's simple enough, we'll take twenty-five up front, twenty-five on the day, and fifty on delivery."

"Okay."

"So let's hear the details."

"Are you familiar with Leapfrog Technologies in Cloverdale?"

They nodded. "Software company, isn't it?" Joe said.

Samantha continued. "That's where I work. I'm the assistant director of new development. We've just developed a new data-mining program for small business applications. It's called Lilypad 5. I want you to steal it and wreck the computer server in a way that will look like an accident."

Tess tapped her manicured fingernails on the table. "You want us to steal a computer program?"

Samantha nodded. "You go in, transfer the program to a portable drive, mess up the server. The next day, everyone thinks there's been some sort of bizarre computer malfunction. No one knows the program is gone. That's what I want."

"So there's only one copy?" Tess asked.

"I know it sounds crazy, but yeah, there's only one right now."

Joe wrote in a small notepad. "I've got a good idea for damaging the server, but I don't know how difficult it'll be to transfer the program."

"No problem," Samantha said. "My nephew, Brandon, is a programmer. He'll go with you to do the transfer. You take care of the in and out and messing up the server."

The workingmen went up to the front counter to pay their bill. Joe scanned the room for other suspicious faces. "Strangers and amateurs. I don't go on the job with them."

"Neither do I. If you screw up the transfer, we'll have nothing. If you highjack the program, I have nothing. So you take Brandon."

Joe smiled. "I'm feeling the love here. Okay, you pay the upfront money; we'll take your boy for a ride." He sipped his coffee. "One more thing. We have to get a look at the ground, so you have to provide Tess with a cover for the duration."

"What do you mean?"

"Tess needs complete access to your offices."

"She'll draw attention to me."

"You need your nephew to transfer the program; I need my partner to scout the job."

Samantha looked at Tess. "Have you got any skills?"

"Not the kind you mean. Don't worry. I know how to look busy."

"Looking busy won't be good enough. We're just the new development group. After a security breach a few years back, the board of directors got paranoid and moved us off of the main campus, so we're a small shop. There has to be a reason you're suddenly there." Samantha closed her eyes and rubbed the bridge of her nose. "What will work? Ah," she opened her eyes and pointed at Tess. "You're a temporary intern from the local college. You know, an adult learner on a job shadow. Brandon can drop you into Orion College's database."

Tess nodded. "Sounds good."

Joe rubbed his chin. "So you're at a separate location? Just how tight is your security?"

"Security counter in the lobby by the elevators, surveillance cameras throughout our offices, random security checks, that's about it." Samantha looked from Tess to Joe. "We done here?"

"Almost." Tess smiled softly, showing her perfect white teeth. "Okay, we know what it is. Now we need to know why."

"Why you're doing it is because I'm paying you."

"But why are *you* doing it?" Tess asked.

"That's none of your business."

"Yes it is. The why is often the reason somebody gets caught. And we're not getting caught."

Samantha looked between them out through the picture window. A yellow front-end loader was scooping up the dirty snow that had been piled up in the back parking lot and was dumping it into a dump truck to be moved across town. "I've been with Leapfrog fifteen years. My boss is a jerk. He always steals credit for what I do, claims my ideas, so I get cheated on bonuses and salary. I'm tired of being a doormat. I just want my fair share. Lilypad 5 has a lot of commercial uses. In the right hands it could also be used for industrial espionage. I'm going to sell it to a competitor."

"Already lined up?" Joe asked.

She nodded.

Joe continued. "So your bosses have been screwing you and now you're going to get paid."

Samantha looked into her empty coffee cup. "That's about the size of it."

"What time do you get to the office in the morning?" Tess asked.

"Eight a.m."

"I'll meet you there. After I look around, I'll know whether it's doable."

Joe and Tess watched Samantha leave the restaurant and trudge across the icy parking lot to her car, a silver Camry. Joe motioned to their waitress, a skinny, gray-blonde woman with a smoker's mouth. "This looks like easy money. A couple of days of light work and we're out of here."

Tess blotted her lips and put her napkin on her plate. "But is it our kind of job?"

"She's not a civilian. She's just another amateur crook who can't go to the police. She sought us out. So ripping her off is fair."

"You believe her reason why?"

"The details? I don't know. It sounds close enough to the truth."

"I got to admit, I feel a little sorry for her."

"Tess, really? She could have filed a lawsuit. She could have changed jobs a long time ago. Instead, she's hiring us to rip them off."

"But she didn't even try to bargain down the hundred thousand."

"But she did negotiate the payment schedule and the job specifics. She's a grown-up making her own decisions."

"What about her company?"

"She's going to rob them, so Lilypad 5 — the data-mining program — is already gone." Joe tapped his fingers on the table as their waitress neared. They stopped talking.

The waitress stopped at their booth. "Anything else?"

"No thanks."

She set their check down, collected the pie plates, and turned away. Tess continued. "You're right, Joe. Samantha made her choices. She's just going to get what she's got coming. But what can I say? There's something about her — I don't know."

Joe nodded. "I understand. You've got feelings. There but for the grace of God, etcetera, etcetera. Let me ask you this. You think she'll change her mind if we don't take this job, or do you think she'll just find somebody else?"

"She'll find somebody else."

"Exactly. So it might as well be us. She won't like it, but she'll have nothing to complain about when we leave with all the cash."

2: The Walk-Through

The next morning, Tess walked into the lobby of the State-to-State Insurance Company Building, a modern steel and glass high-rise in downtown Cloverdale. She was wearing her college intern outfit: a well-worn, cream-colored, knee-length down coat that she'd bought at Goodwill just for this job, a cobalt blue cardigan sweater over a matching V-neck t-shirt, a tan skirt, and brown, calf-high, high-heeled boots. She hoped she looked sexy enough to put the men at ease, while not looking like competition to the other women. That was the look she was striving for—the look that would give her the benefit of the doubt with all the employees in the office. To her left was a Wholly Roasters Coffee Shop, where a long line of office workers—men and women in a mix of suits and various levels of work-casual clothing—were getting their last personally chosen cups of coffee for the morning. To her right was a branch of Family Savings Bank, ATM open twenty-four hours. In front of her were three elevators and a counter manned by a blue-uniformed security guard, no gun visible. A sign next to the elevators indicated that the first and second floors were occupied by Genius Travel Consultants; the third, fourth, and fifth floors by Leapfrog Technologies; and the sixth through fifteenth floors by the State-to-State Insurance Company.

Samantha, dressed in a brown skirt suit with a white blouse that fit her just as snugly as the gray suit she'd been wearing at Perkins, was waiting for her by the security counter. "Tess." They shook hands. "Any trouble finding your way?"

"No, Ms. Bartel, no problem."

"Call me Samantha." She motioned toward the counter. The security guard, a muscled-up twenty-something with a blond buzz cut and a close shave, pushed a clipboard toward her. "You need to fill out this form for a security ID, ma'am. Everyone at Leapfrog wears one."

Tess filled in the form. The guard said, "Look over here," and took her picture. A few minutes later, he handed her a photo ID to clip onto her sweater.

Samantha pointed to the elevators. "The far left one is our dedicated elevator. Let's go upstairs and get you settled in. I'm sure you're dying to get started."

While they were alone in the elevator, Tess asked, "So you've got your own elevator?"

"Lets us control security from the lobby."

"How does that work?"

"Genius and State-to-State contract with us to control elevator access to their floors and supply surveillance of the lobby and parking deck. We need more security than they do and it's simpler than everyone running their own."

"The bank and the coffee place?"

"They're on their own. They're locked up tight at five p.m., and the bank is supposed to have a special alarm system."

"Can you go from the parking deck next door straight into Leapfrog?"

"You need a key. The deck brings you into the third floor. We have stairs inside our offices and permanent employees have elevator security fobs to access the fourth and fifth floors via the elevator."

"Where's your office?"

"Fifth floor."

"So you enter the building from the parking deck on the third floor and use your fob to access the fifth floor."

She nodded. "Unless I need to see someone on the third floor."

"Who's there?"

"Reception, some of the techs."

"Fifth floor is management?"

"And team leaders, the conference room."

"Fourth floor?"

"Programmers and the server room."

They got off the elevator at the third floor. The room was painted sage green; the carpet was a mottled brown. To the left were two overstuffed tan leather chairs and a glass-topped coffee table with several magazines spread across it. To the right, a thin, middle-aged woman wearing jeans with a scooped-neck white shirt and a wine-colored corduroy jacket sat at a glass-topped desk with a computer workstation to one side. "Carol," Samantha said. "This is Tess. She's a temporary intern from Orion College."

Carol used one finger to push her wire-framed glasses up her nose. "Hello, Tess."

"Hi."

"If you need anything," Samantha continued, "Carol's the person to see."

Carol rolled her eyes and smoothed her dark gray hair back behind her ears. "I'll do what I can, dear."

They walked back through a large doorway into a room that was divided into fabric-lined cubicles. Several young men and women dressed in jeans and hoodies or turtlenecks already sat in front of their computers, intent on their screens. At the end of the room was a gray steel stairwell. Tess glanced around. Security cameras were located at the doorway and the stairwell. They started up the stairs. Tess whispered, "Where does the video feed to?"

"Screens are behind the counter in the lobby. Cameras from the parking deck as well. Is that a problem?"

Tess shook her head.

On the fourth floor, there was the same configuration of security cameras, but the layout was different. On one side of the sage green room was another row of cubicles, but on the other side was a row of offices. "Servers are in the center office. The other rooms are supply storage and offices for senior pro-grammers."

"Your nephew up here?"

"He's in a cubicle."

They continued up to the fifth floor, where there was a sage green hallway with doors on both sides, most of them open. Ronnie Franklin stood in the hallway talking with Leroy Smalls, the head of security. Franklin was forty-seven years old, just under six feet, slim, with close-cropped dark hair and a Van Dyke beard. He wore dark blue jeans, a white button-down shirt, and a necktie with Daffy Duck on it. Smalls was a heavy set, sixty-three-year-old black man, just over six feet tall, with a shaved head. He was a retired police detective. He wore a blue blazer, white shirt with striped tie, and gray slacks. Even though Franklin was only a few inches shorter, Smalls seemed to tower over him. Smalls had just finished telling a joke. Franklin's hand covered his mouth and beard as if he were trying to muffle his laugh, while Smalls's deep chuckle reverberated down the hallway.

"Samantha," Smalls said, "good morning." He looked Tess over with his cop eye. "I don't believe we've met."

"Tess," Samantha said, "this is Leroy Smalls, our security chief, and Ronnie Franklin, the director of new development."

"Mr. Smalls, Mr. Franklin, pleased to meet you."

Samantha continued. "Tess is a temporary intern from Orion College. She's doing a job shadow of me for her — what is it?"

"Management class," Tess said.

Smalls nodded. "If I can help you in any way, let me know." He turned to Samantha. "I don't want to cramp your style, Sam, but it's limited access until the background check comes through."

"Of course, Leroy. It shouldn't be a problem."

Smalls walked down the hall to the elevator. Franklin looked Tess up and down and smiled knowingly. "Temporary intern? I hope you're around here long enough for us to get to know you."

Tess shifted her weight to accentuate her curves, and smiled with her eyes in a way that said *I hope so, too*. Franklin's gaze drifted to her cleavage. She turned to Samantha. "What's next, boss?"

Samantha pointed toward a door. "Hang up your coat in my office. There should be a report ready for me downstairs. Could you go get it?"

Tess hung up her coat and then disappeared down the stairs. Franklin watched her go. "Jesus, Sammy, she's a hot one. The staff gets a look at her and they're going to believe that rumor you're a lesbian." He sniggered as he walked away.

Samantha turned toward her office. The corners of her mouth dropped. "Asshole," she muttered, even though she was more irritated with herself than she was with him. After all these years, why did his juvenile needling still get to her?

At 6:30 p.m., Franklin was eating dinner with his family in the dining room of their two-story home in Clareview Heights, an upscale neighborhood on the south side of Cloverdale. They were gathered at one end of a long walnut dining room table, Franklin at the head, his wife, Melanie, to his left and his daughter, Kat, to his right. Melanie was a short, plump woman with salon-dyed, dark brown, curly hair, and a loud speaking voice. Kat was tall and thin, with shoulder-length light brown hair, a perfect nose, and tiny frown lines at the corners of her mouth. She was dressed in the high school dance team's blue and gold practice clothes. White take-out cartons of grilled salmon with orange cream sauce, roast potatoes, and asparagus salad that Melanie had picked up from Justin's Cafe on the way home from her manicure sat out on the table in front of them.

"Anyway, Ronnie," Melanie said as she pushed up the sleeves of her plum-colored velour tracksuit, "the lease on the BMW is up in two months—"

"I know," he interrupted. He looked at his daughter. "Could you pass the potatoes?"

Kat picked up the take-out carton of roasted potatoes and set it down within his reach. Franklin spooned potatoes onto his plate. "I'm sorry to be short, dear. It's been a rough day. What's your point?"

Melanie reached over and patted his hand. "I'd like a car that's a little bigger next time."

"Bigger?"

"You know, with more room to turn around in."

"What? Like an SUV?"

"It doesn't have to be an SUV, just something more sub-stantial than the 328."

Franklin shrugged sympathetically and ate a forkful of salmon. "This salmon's great."

"They always do a great job at Justin's."

He turned to his daughter. "Don't you have the Europe trip this spring?"

Kat nodded. "Spring break. I'm going to need some clothes and a new suitcase."

"And you still haven't told us what you want for your birthday."

She looked down at her plate and pushed her potatoes around with her fork. Her hair hung down in her face. "I really haven't had time to think about it."

Melanie reached for her wine glass. "You need to tell us pretty soon if you want it on time."

Kat looked at her smartphone. "May I be excused? Grace is in the driveway."

"What are you two up to?" Franklin asked.

A car horn sounded. "Dad. Duh." She pointed at her clothes. "Dance team practice; then a study session at Karen's."

"What about flute practice?"

"Got in an hour before dinner, Dad."

"Don't be out too late," Melanie said.

Kat took her plate and glass to the kitchen. Melanie yelled after her, "Drink your milk."

Franklin heard the kitchen door shut and the garage open. "You know she's hoping for a car of her own for her birthday."

"I know. I've been thinking about models. Something sporty. A convertible, maybe," Melanie said.

"Money's tight right now."

"What? A car's not that much, something American made. We can trade in the old van."

"If her heart is set on a car, she'll have to take a rain check. When the new data-mining program we've been working on rolls out, the stock will go up and I can cash some in. Besides, there'll probably be a bonus."

Melanie downed the rest of her wine. "You're just being cheap."

"That's not fair." Franklin pushed away from the table without finishing his food.

"What about dessert? I got the carrot cake you like from Ostell's Bakery."

"Later." He tried to sound as if he wasn't irritated. "Thanks for a great meal. I'm going up to my office for a little while."

"Don't forget I've got cards at Jody's."

"Oh, yeah." He leaned over and kissed her. "Have fun."

He went up the thickly carpeted stairs to his office, a small bedroom that contained an old oak desk and a twenty-year-old stereo system on a matching credenza. He opened his laptop, glanced through some news websites, and then settled into a game of solitaire. Money, money, money. Spending money. Buying bright, shiny toys. That's all Melanie thought about and that's exactly what Kat had learned at her knee. It took all of his paycheck to keep up with the payments every month. Lilypad 5 needed to be a giant success if he were going to keep his head above water. A giant success with a big bonus attached. Leapfrog stock climbing into the stratosphere. That's all that could possibly save him. Samantha had to get the job done. His cell phone rang. He fished it out of his pocket. It was Angie, his girlfriend. He put the phone up to his ear. "Yeah?"

"Hey, baby, is this a good time?"

"Uh-huh. How are you?"

"You miss me?"

"Every hour of every day."

She laughed and he wished she were there in the room with him. "I bought a new lingerie set. I'm just trying it on in front of the mirror. Just wait 'til you see it."

"You're killing me."

"I bet. Why don't you just slip on over here? Sneak out the window."

"I could make a quick visit."

"Not too quick."

He glanced at his watch. "Kat's at dance team practice and Melanie ought to be leaving in the next ten minutes."

"Come on over. The door's unlocked."

Leroy Smalls, still dressed from work, shook the ice in the bottom of his rum and coke. The bartender, a dreadlocked black man of about thirty, the sleeves of his white shirt rolled up to his elbows, nodded and reached for the glass. "Getting late for you, Pops?"

Smalls shrugged. "One more, James. I want to hear the talking heads go over that game."

All in one smooth motion, James smiled, shook his head, and reached for the rum in the well under the bar. "You got to start rooting for winners."

Smalls turned back to the TV hanging on the wall behind the bar. He and James were the only black faces in the Ace-King-Queen Sports Bar on a Thursday night. It was the typical strip mall venue: sports posters and paraphernalia hanging on the walls, TVs positioned so that every seat was a good seat. There were three other men at the bar, and five or six tables of younger men and women drinking pitchers of beer. Only two of the tables were making any noise at all. A slow night. That's why he liked to come here. Easy to hear the game. The commentators were talking, but he wasn't listening. James set the fresh drink in front of him. Smalls tallied up his losses: $200 on the Celtics game, plus the $700 he was down from the football play-offs. What had he dropped on the Rose Bowl? It must have been $150. He was in a bad patch. He'd been comfortably ahead after the World Series; the world would turn and he'd get ahead again. He took out his phone and speed-dialed his bookie. "Hey, Gary, it's Smalls."

"Leroy, I was hoping to hear from you."

Smalls pulled a scrap of paper from his shirt pocket. "I want to lay my bets for the weekend."

"Leroy, I'm sorry, buddy, but I can't carry you any further. You got to pay to play."

"Let me work the weekend, and I'll square up with you next week."

"Tell you what I'll do. You pay upfront for any new bets, and I'll carry what you owe until next week. Just stop by the house. I'll even take a check."

Smalls took a sip from his drink. "Gary, you know I'm good for it."

"Sure, I know you're good for it, but management doesn't like cops, even retired cops, too far behind. What they going to do, break a cop's leg?"

A woman in her mid-thirties, her red hair pulled back in a ponytail and an oversized Atlanta Hawks jersey slipping down her shoulder to expose a black bra strap, came up to the bar, raised a hand toward James and gave Smalls a quick nod.

Smalls turned away from her. "Gary, I don't want to have to take my trade somewhere else. Just see me through the weekend and I'll pay everything I owe."

Gary sighed. "Okay, Leroy, I'll carry you myself through the weekend. But that's the end of it. New slate on Monday. That's the nine hundred plus or minus whatever happens this weekend."

"Thanks, brother."

"So what's your action?"

Joe and Tess turned off the boulevard into the parking lot of Lake Ryan, the old skating rink and city park in the run-down northeast section of Cloverdale. The wind had increased since the sun had set, and gusts blew the dry snow up into snow devils. The skating rink had been closed three years ago when the indoor rink opened at the new mall in the southeast, and the park was little used in winter. The parks and rec department plowed the parking lot once after Christmas for the occasional hiker, but snow had drifted into dunes since then. Joe wheeled their blue Ford Explorer around the deeper drifts, working his way to the back end of the parking lot away from the boulevard and the streetlights. He backed into a spot on the far side from the trailhead and put the Explorer into park. "Ready to play?"

"Always." Tess adjusted her pink stocking cap, but she kept her eyes on the entry to the parking lot. "How much do you think we can squeeze out of Bartel?"

"Who knows? If we actually rip her off after the job, we might get near two hundred thousand. Remember that guy who owned — what was it? Ah, Manhattan Menswear."

"That was sweet. But guys that greedy and stupid don't stumble into our path every day."

He patted her gloved hand. "All the same, she might be susceptible to my many charms or she might be a switch-hitter or her nephew might be liable to give up the game for the right kind of attention. We've just got to be flexible. There's no way of telling where we might find an opening." He squeezed her hand. "By the by, have I told you today how beautiful you look in your Goodwill down coat?"

Her teeth flashed in the dark as she smiled. "You better tighten up your game, baby. Your insincerity is showing."

A silver Camry turned into the parking lot, wove through the snowdrifts, and pulled up next to them. Samantha and her nephew Brandon hopped out and climbed into the backseat of the Explorer. Joe and Tess turned in their seats to face them. Brandon was twenty-six years old, thin and soft, with short brown hair and round framed glasses. He wore a thigh-length, brown leather coat with a faux sheepskin lining. Samantha wore a thick down coat and furry boots.

"Did we have to meet out here?" Samantha rubbed her hands together. "This has got to be the coldest place in town."

"So this is your nephew?" Joe asked.

She nodded. "Yeah."

"He know what's up?"

She crossed her arms against the cold. "He knows what he needs to do."

Tess studied him in the back seat. "Good to meet you, Brandon." He gave her a practiced bored look.

Samantha looked from Tess to Joe. "So, are we on?"

Tess nodded. "It's doable. The only real problem is getting past the guard in the lobby. The rest of it is standard alarms and video surveillance."

"Okay," Samantha said, "but it has to be completely quiet, so everyone will think it was a freak accident."

"I'm going to overheat the computer," Joe said, "so it burns itself up."

Brandon perked up. "Will that work?"

"Worked when I tested it."

Brandon continued. "The guard walks the outside of the building and up through the parking garage on the hour."

"Really?" Tess said. "He should be manning the security monitors."

"CEO ordered it. Somebody keyed his Mercedes when he was visiting one time, so he wants to discourage the" — Brandon held up his hands to make quote marks — "'bad element.'"

Joe grinned. "We'll check it out."

Samantha fished a pay-as-you-go cell phone out of her coat pocket. "When the deed is done, call me on this phone. Brandon can bring me the program."

"Brandon going to be carrying our money?" Joe asked.

"You get your money after I sell the program."

Joe shook his head. "Then we're going to the buyer together. We're not letting the merchandise out of sight until we're paid off. If you can't pay us out of your own pocket, we're along for the ride. So you need to tell us who the buyer is."

"And then you rip me off and go to the buyer on your own?"

"How could we do that? The buyer doesn't know us."

"We all have trust issues," Samantha said. "All I'll tell you now is that he's a small-time Steve Jobs wannabe looking for a shortcut up the ladder."

"Fair enough," Joe said.

"So call me when it's done." Samantha started to open the door. A blast of icy air shot into the car.

"Aren't you forgetting something?" Joe said. "The clock starts ticking when we get our twenty-five grand."

Samantha shut her door, reached in her coat, pulled out an accordion envelope, and passed it to Joe. He thumbed through the money inside. "Excellent." He looked up at Brandon. "I need your phone number."

Brandon scribbled his phone number on a scrap of paper and passed it up. "When are we going to do it?"

"Tomorrow, if the pieces of the puzzle fall together."

"Tomorrow? That soon? How can you be ready that fast?"

Joe looked at Samantha. "You said he was up for this." Before she could answer, he turned to Brandon. "You going to need an adult diaper or are you good to go?"

"I'm good to go."

"We won't be babysitting."

"I'll pull my weight."

Joe frowned, his mustache curling down the sides of his mouth. "Let's be clear. I won't go to jail because you froze up. If you're not up to the challenge, we'll leave you there."

"I can do it."

"Okay, then. You'll hear from me in the morning if it's a go."

"Anything else?" Samantha asked.

"No."

"Then call me when it's done." She pushed open the door.

Joe and Tess watched the Camry meander back through the snowdrifts in the parking lot and turn out onto the boulevard. Tess picked up the envelope containing the $25,000 off the console and shoved it into her coat pocket. "You know, she was hoping you wouldn't ask for the money."

"Yes, she was. And she didn't flinch when I pressed the kid. She's tougher than she looks. What do you think of the kid?"

"He's way geeky, but he likes women. Might be a little young for me to work, though."

"Tess, that boy wouldn't stand a chance if you put on a charm offensive."

"I wouldn't want him to see me naked in a bright light is all I'm saying."

"It's just mind over matter. It's not going to come to that anyway. This is just a dine and dash."

"What about Samantha? Think you can charm her?"

"I don't think Samantha thinks I'm her type, so we may be working for a living this time around if we want to scrape up all the loose money. Worst case, we take our hundred grand and go."

"Not a bad piece of change."

"Not bad at all. Let's go back over to the State-to-State Building and see what we can find out about the security." He put the Explorer in gear and started rolling across the parking lot.

"Really think we'll be ready tomorrow?" Tess asked.

"Why not? This is just regular burglary tools, security uniforms, spray accelerant, move a couple of cars around, depending on what we see tonight."

3: Destroying the Server

On Friday afternoon, after work, Samantha sat on a wooden stool at a bar-height round table in the PourAway Coffee Shop on Orion Street in the college district. The interior was fake Tudor stucco and dark brown timber; the crowd was a mixture of animated college students planning their evenings and older, bone-tired professors looking for that last jolt to carry them home to an early bedtime. There was some pleasant alternative rock music playing over the sound system, but Samantha didn't know the band. She was dressed from the office in a navy skirt, pink button-up blouse, and a dark blue cardigan sweater. Her gray wool coat and black handbag sat on the stool next to her.

She glanced at her watch and then at the front door. She shifted her weight and took a sip of Earl Grey tea. She was waiting for a man she had met through an online dating service for managers and professionals. She hadn't bothered to print out the page with the man's picture on it, and she was having a little trouble remembering his distinguishing characteristics. All the middle-aged men who came in the door were a little gray, a little balding, and a little bit soft—not that any of that mattered to her. Her bathing suit days were long behind her. Usually the men were at the first meeting place before she was, waving at her when she came through the door. She'd never been to a first meeting where the man was late, and she was beginning to believe he'd gotten cold feet. She took another sip of tea. The door opened. A man shuffled in, stoop-shouldered, closer to sixty than fifty, his hair more white than gray, his suit worn as casually as a set of work clothes. When he saw her he waved and smiled. She smiled back. His picture on the website must

19

have been ten years old. What did that mean? Vanity or lack of confidence?

"Hello," he said. "You must be Samantha. I'm Reuben." He stuck out his hand. She shook it. His grip was firm; his skin was smooth.

She smiled. "Pleased to meet you."

"Sorry I'm late. Had a meeting with a student that went over; didn't have your phone number with me." He sat on the stool opposite her. "Hope I didn't keep you too long."

She smiled. "No, no, that's okay."

"I see you've got something. Let me get a cup of coffee." He shuffled off to the counter and returned with a steaming mug. "They know me here." He sat back down. "So tell me about yourself. I read your profile, but it's been a long day. Let's see—I know you've never been married, that you work for a tech company. Are you an office assistant?"

"Manager."

"Oh, I'm sorry. Your clothes—"

"Small software companies tend to be informal."

"Do you like what you do?"

She shrugged. "Yes, usually. Some days are more challenging than others. What about you? You're a professor, right?"

He nodded. "It's all I've ever been and all I ever wanted to be."

"So you enjoy teaching, working with students?"

"I don't do much teaching. Mainly I do research on small mammals. Spend the summer out in the field and the fall and spring in the lab." He drank some coffee. "What does a manager do at a software company?"

"Well, I'm the assistant director of new development. So I coordinate a group of programmers working to develop new products. It can be hit or miss. But when we've got a product that looks more than promising, it's pretty exciting."

"Long hours?"

"Yeah, it can be." She nodded. "Same for you?"

"Definitely. But when you love what you do—" he shrugged.

"And what did your wife do?"

"She was trained in zoology, but she mainly raised our kids and organized our lives. Before she got sick, she came with me in the summer. When the kids were at home, they came, too."

"When you wrote that you enjoyed spending time at the beach and traveling in foreign countries, I thought you were doing that in the summer."

"No, no. That's going to international scientific meetings. And we did take the kids to the beach for a week a few summers. It was a lot of fun."

"So, what are you looking for—someone to take your wife's place?"

He shook his head. "I won't lie to you. When I first started dating, that's exactly what I was doing. I wasn't really over my grief. You can imagine how well that worked. But I finally made my peace. No one could replace Martha. And times have changed. I like to think that I've changed with them. I'm looking for a companion. Someone to be with for the rest of our lives."

"Someone to be with after work?"

"Exactly. An independent person who enjoys her own work; doesn't want to be crowded by me."

"Do you have any idea what you'll do when you retire?"

"I don't plan to retire. I already do what I want everyday."

Samantha sipped her tea. She wasn't expecting to be swept off her feet. He seemed like a reasonable guy. Wasn't grabby, seemed to know what he wanted. But why hadn't he talked about his kids? Parents always talk about their kids. Or was that just an excuse? What exactly was she looking for? Where was the line between caretaking and companionship? Maybe she should give him a chance. Maybe his kids were interesting, fun people. But why did she have a gut feeling that if she ended up with this man, her life would be just as empty as it was now, only with twice the laundry and cleaning? Surely she had the right to expect a man who would turn a little toward her?

Her cup was empty. She'd planned this date to be her alibi if the Lilypad theft went wrong, but it was already clear that this date was a waste of time. "Reuben, you seem like a great guy, but I'm looking for somebody with a little more room in his life."

"From just a few minutes' talk, how can you tell how much room is in my life?"

She held her hand up. "I'm not here to argue. I've made up my mind."

His eyes lost their confidence. He looked down at his coffee cup.

She set her handbag on the table and slipped on her wool coat. "Like I said, you seem like a great guy, so let me play manager for a few minutes." He cocked his head. "When you show up late—no matter how good the reason—talk about how much you love your work and say you'll never retire, well, that's less available time than most people want. Don't take this the wrong way, but maybe your online profile should better describe your interests. Play up who you really are. You might get less first meetings, but they might last longer." She looked at his face without looking him in the eyes. "I'm sure there are women looking to have a relationship in their spare time. I'm just not one of them. Good luck." She picked up her handbag and meandered through the tables to the door.

Joe, Tess, and Brandon sat in the dark in a stolen green Suburban in the row of cars left in the on-street parking across from the State-to-State Insurance Company Building in downtown Cloverdale. The lights in the glass-walled lobby were on. The Wholly Roasters Coffee Shop and Family Savings Bank branch in the lobby had been closed since 5:00 p.m. The sidewalks in this part of the downtown were deserted. No one walked in this weather. The bitter cold made the light from the streetlamps seem hard and contained, as if the lit areas were separate rooms marked out on the street. The occasional car that drove by headed for the strip of restaurants and bars three blocks away sounded loud and lonely in the cold dark. Brandon sat in the back seat, hugging himself in his blue security guard parka. "Why can't we have the heat on?"

Joe, his parka hood up, spoke over his shoulder. "Car exhaust coming from a parked car shows in the cold air. Attracts too much attention."

Tess sat in the passenger's side front seat looking through a pair of high-powered field glasses, watching the security guard at the counter by the elevators in the lobby. He was a fat kid with a dark crew cut and black-rimmed glasses. "We're in luck. We caught the doughnut man. A toddler could outrun this guy." She glanced at her watch. "Only a few more minutes now."

A red Prius pulled to the curb in front of the State-to-State Insurance Company Building. The passenger, a man in a heavy, tan parka, hopped out and scurried toward the building. "What's going on?" Joe asked.

"Hold on," Tess replied.

The man jogged up the sidewalk on the right side of the building and stopped at the Family Savings Bank ATM.

"He's just getting cash," Tess said.

Meanwhile, the security guard pulled on his parka, tugged on his gloves, and checked his flashlight. At exactly 9:00 p.m., he walked out the front door and started down the sidewalk to the left toward the parking deck. Joe glanced from the security guard to the man at the ATM. "Come on, come on," he muttered.

The man jogged back to the Prius. The security guard turned up into the parking deck. Joe looked at his watch. "Okay," Joe said, "we've got twelve minutes to clear the lobby. Let's go."

They got out of the Suburban and hurried across the street, their shoes crunching on the compacted snow. They were all wearing dark blue parkas, blue pants, and black work shoes just like the security guard's, hoods up, faces obscured by shadow. Tess carried a black shoulder bag that held the tools Joe had chosen for the job. Joe squatted in front of the deadbolt on the glass doors, pulled off his gloves, knelt on them, and reached for his lock picks in his inside pocket. Tess and Brandon stood behind him to shield him from passersby.

A few moments later, the bolt slipped back. He put his gloves on, pushed through the door, moved quietly across the lobby, and sat down at the desk behind the security counter. He glanced at the security camera monitors. The guard was still walking through the second floor of the parking deck. Joe turned off the lobby camera and motioned to Tess and Brandon. Tess bolted the front door behind them. She and Brandon went directly to the elevator. Joe found some elevator security fobs in a wooden box on a shelf behind the counter and tossed one to her. The elevator doors opened. She got into the elevator, Brandon at her heels, waved the fob in front of the electronic eye and pressed the fourth floor button. Joe focused his attention on the computer controlling the security cameras. He turned off the fourth floor cameras and the camera to the door to the third floor parking deck, and rigged the monitors to show static pictures on the screens. Then for good measure, he input a command to randomly interweave the footage from all the cameras as they recorded.

The guard was testing the first floor doors from the parking deck into Genius Travel Consultants when Joe deleted the footage of himself crossing the lobby and turned the lobby camera back on. He put the chair back the way he found it, grabbed a security fob from the box, slipped along the wall to stay out of camera view and punched the "up" button on the elevator. He could see the security guard walking down the ramp of the parking deck. He was hunched down in his coat, his flashlight angled toward the sidewalk in front of him. Joe stepped back against the elevator door to make himself more difficult to see. The elevator door opened. Should he take the elevator or the stairs? Joe could see the guard leaving the parking deck and starting down the sidewalk to the front of the building. He studied the guard, watching his mannerisms, trying to decide if the guard would be back in the lobby in time to notice that the elevator was going up. "Stop calculating," Joe muttered. He used the fob, punched the fourth floor button, and went up in the elevator.

Up on the fourth floor, Tess and Brandon were already in the server room. The server room was a ten by twelve foot office, sage green like all the rest, where four computer servers sat side by side on a long metal table in the middle of the room. These four servers were networked to all of Leapfrog's computers in the building. Brandon sat next to the far right server, hunched over a tablet computer that lay across his thighs, latex gloves on his hands, copying Lilypad 5. When they heard the elevator door open out in the hallway, Brandon glanced over his shoulder to look at the door and pulled up the hood on his coat while Tess stepped over to the wall beside the door with a Taser in her hand. They heard footsteps approaching. Tess raised the Taser to shoulder height. Brandon saw Joe in the doorway and nodded. Tess put the Taser back in her coat pocket. Joe touched her shoulder as he passed her; then leaned down next to Brandon and whispered, "How much longer? Doughnut boy is already back."

"Just a few more minutes. Took longer to input the security codes with these gloves on than I thought it would."

Down in the lobby, the security guard was hanging up his parka. He poured himself a fresh cup of coffee, sat down at the desk behind the counter, and scooted his chair up. The chair, the computer keyboard, the login clipboard—they all seemed just a little out of position. He looked at the security camera monitors. Why was the monitor for the third floor door to the parking deck blipping in that annoying way? He sipped his coffee, and then held his hands around the hot cup to warm his fingers. He glanced at the monitors. Everything was fine, except for that blipping. He looked in the desk drawer for the manual, but he couldn't find it. How hard could it be? He got on the computer and opened the third floor door security camera. It wasn't recording. Weird. He wondered if it had been turned off all day. He turned it back on and then checked the monitor. The blipping had stopped.

In the server room, Brandon had pulled the server from its case, exposing the circuit boards and the hard drive. Joe shoved a pencil into the fan box to stop the fan blades from turning. He looked back at Tess. "Give me the can."

She reached into the black shoulder bag and handed him an aerosol can of accelerant. He sprayed the circuit boards and hard drive before he sprayed the fan motor. He pulled the pencil out of the fan box. The fan blades wobbled three hundred degrees and stopped. The fan motor started to smoke. "Close it up."

Brandon looked at him quizzically. "That's going to do it?"

"Leave the computer on and it'll overheat and melt the boards and wreck the hard drive in five minutes."

"Won't it leave some sort of residue?"

"It'll burn off clean. They won't see a thing."

Brandon slid the server back into its case.

"What about the other three?" Joe asked.

"Not involved."

Tess put the accelerant back in her shoulder bag. "Let's get out of here."

They locked the door to the server room and took the elevator down to the third floor.

In the lobby, the security guard was checking all the video cameras to make sure they were recording. Lobby was fine, third floor was fine, fourth floor was out. Stranger than strange. He clicked on the icon to turn the camera back on. While he was doing that, he didn't see the three security parkas leaving the building on the monitor that showed the third floor door to the parking deck. He finished checking the rest of the cameras. They were all on now. He made a note in the security logs on his clipboard. After he finished updating the log, he stood up, set his coffee cup down next to the coffee pot, stretched, and went to the lobby men's room. When he got back to the security counter and sat down, he saw that the silent fire alarm in the fourth floor server room had tripped. The cameras showed a thin smoke creeping under the door. He jumped to his feet, pulled the building fire alarm next to the elevator doors, and snatched up the phone.

"911 emergency."

"There's a fire at the State-to-State Insurance Building."

"Fire? Who am I speaking with?"

"Gregory with the Leapfrog Technologies security team."

"Anyone in the building?"

"Nobody's here."

"Fire and rescue is on the way."

"I'm going to hang up."

"Are you sure the building is empty?"

"Definitely."

"Get out of the building. Wait for the first responders."

Joe, Tess, and Brandon drove out of the exit to the parking deck on the far side from the State-to-State Insurance Building in a stolen Toyota Corolla that they had left there earlier. As they drove into the downtown, they heard the sirens of a fire truck, followed by the long horn as it rolled through an intersection. "Wow," Brandon said, "the fire response time is fast. Will the fire have done enough damage?"

"Relax. Only takes a couple of minutes," Joe said.

Tess turned in her seat to look at Brandon in the back. "You did a good job. Didn't clutch up at all."

"There wasn't much to it."

"You'd be surprised how many people can't perform even simple tasks when the pressure is on. It's woulda, coulda, shoulda instead of getting the job done."

Joe glanced in the rearview mirror. "Where do we drop you?"

"Take the next right, go one block, take a left. My car's the grey-blue Civic."

Joe made the turn. The Colossus Bar and Restaurant was in the middle of the block on the right. Cars lined both sides of the street, some covered with a thin layer of snow. The driving lane was narrow. Joe slowed down. A police car turned from the right and started toward them. Joe glanced in the rearview mirror. All clear. The police car turned on its lights and siren. Brandon reached for the door handle. "Take a breath, kid," Joe said. Joe pulled in close to a black Cadillac on the right and stopped. The police car squeezed past them and kept on going.

Brandon turned in his seat to watch the lights disappear at the corner. "Jesus."

Joe chuckled. "Guilty conscience?" He continued down the block and made a left turn. Up ahead, parked on the right, was Brandon's old Civic, covered in snow. Joe pulled over. "The tablet stays with us."

Brandon shrugged. "Sure." He passed the tablet computer up to Tess, who put it in the black tool bag. "What about the coat?"

"Leave it in the car."

Brandon took off the security guard parka and put on his leather coat. "See you later."

"Get your alibi set. And get rid of the pants and shoes in a dumpster far away from your house. Do it tonight."

"Okay, okay. I'll get it done." Brandon got out of the Corolla. The icy wind stung his face. While he reached in his pocket for his car keys, he felt for the thumb drive that contained the copy he'd made of Lilypad 5. It was there in the bottom of his pocket.

Samantha sat in a bubble bath in her candle-lit bathroom, listening to the smooth jazz program on public radio, a glass of pinot grigio in her hand. Why hadn't she gone out to dinner with Reuben? Why did everything about dating have to be so serious? So what if he wasn't a keeper? She'd missed an opportunity to work on her dating skills. She set the glass on the rim of the tub, lay back in the water, and put a damp washcloth on her face. Was she really so desperate to find a mate? Was she afraid that if she just went on some casual dates she'd be slowly pulled into some man's orbit and would just settle rather than keep on looking? She nodded to herself. Of course she was. It was the story of her life. Settling for second best, unwilling to make the effort to find something better, something she deserved.

Look at her career. When she finished college, she didn't want to move too far away from her parents because they were in poor health, so she took the job with Leapfrog. Always promised herself she'd find a better job. Now she was past her prime. She couldn't keep up technically with the youngsters anymore. She'd wasted her youth working fourteen-hour days. Now she had no husband and no kids. She dropped the washcloth into the water, sat up, and sipped her wine. Men always got the credit. Ronnie had never had an original idea in his life, but he was the master at spreading blame. All these years, she'd told herself she'd been working like a dog for the great retirement she was going to have, and now her retirement was dependent on Leapfrog's stock price, and the stock price was dependent on the success of Lilypad 5, and Lilypad 5 was a buggy mess. But Ronnie couldn't admit that to the board of directors because without Lilypad, Leapfrog was headed for bankruptcy.

She sighed. She should have left five years ago when the board forced out Rudy and Dave. They started the company. They knew how to innovate. Instead, to keep from being fired for incompetence, she'd hired thieves to sabotage Lilypad so her team would get a few more months to fix its flaws and make it into the success they all needed it to be. She shook her head. How much lower could she go? Well, she'd given her life to those bastards. There was no right or wrong, just haves and have-nots. The company would set her out in the dumpster in a minute. She had to take care of herself as best she could.

The throwaway cell phone rang. She set her wine down on the rim of the tub and picked up the phone. "Yes?"

Tess said, "It's all good. See you tomorrow."

Samantha set the phone down on the rim of the tub, drank off her wine, and opened the bathtub drain. Step one was done. She leaned back in the tub, enjoying the candlelight while the water ran out. Maybe the plan really was going to work. She stood up, pulled the shower curtain, and turned on the shower to rinse off, letting the shower put out the candles. When she turned off the shower and opened the curtain, the only light in the bathroom fell through the open door from the bedroom.

Leroy Smalls, Ronnie Franklin, and Stuart Jackson, the CEO of Leapfrog Technologies, stood in the lobby of Leapfrog's offices on the third floor of the State-to-State Insurance Building. Smalls, who had come from a sports bar when Gregory called him, was still wearing his gray slacks, blue blazer, and striped tie. Ronnie Franklin was wearing a red and white striped pajama top with sweatpants and running shoes. His hair and beard were mussed as if he'd been in bed. Stuart Jackson was wearing charcoal pinstripe suit pants and a wrinkled white shirt with no necktie, but his sandy gray hair was carefully combed and his eyes looked alert behind his steel-rimmed glasses. The firefighters were gone. The third floor was undamaged, except for the smell of smoke. On the fourth floor, only the server room had any actual damage, though the smell of fried electronics was stronger all down the hall and up the stairwell, and the carpets were badly tracked from the firefighters' boots. Jackson sat down on one of the overstuffed tan leather chairs and looked through the glass-topped coffee table at his own black dress shoes. "What do we know, Leroy?"

Smalls glanced at Franklin, and then looked down at Jackson. "Fire and Rescue think it was some sort of freak electrical accident. Server overheated. I'll follow up with them on Monday, when the technical people are back at the main office, but that's all we got for now."

Jackson slowly nodded his head, but he didn't look up. "There hasn't been anything strange going on around here has there? Anyone who's developed bad habits or has been acting peculiar?"

Franklin cut in. "Samantha has seemed a little jumpy lately, but that's probably just nerves about the roll-out."

Smalls gave Franklin a "stop-talking-crazy" look and then turned back to Jackson. "There's nothing to suggest sabotage, unless Fire and Rescue says different. Everybody's clean as a whistle. We finished quarterly checks last week. Samantha just started an intern, but I've had eyes on her the whole time she's been in the building."

"What about the security cameras?"

"The computer went on the fritz sometime today. The footage is a mess. It'll take some time to sort it out and even then I don't know if it will tell us anything. I'm putting in a new computer tomorrow."

"That doesn't sound like a coincidence."

"I'm on it with both feet, Stuart. If there's anything crooked going on, I'll find it out."

"Stay on it. We can't have any more mistakes." Jackson took off his glasses and ran his free hand over his face. "So, Ronnie, let's have the bad news. What projects were affected?"

Franklin shrugged. "Looks like Lilypad was fried."

Jackson's head shot up. "Lilypad? Jesus Christ. What about the earlier versions? Or the copy?"

"The versions without glitches and dead ends had all been transferred to the main server as part of the security protocol. And the copy? I don't know what happened there. It should have been safe on the other server, but it appears to be an incomplete mess."

Jackson turned to Smalls. "Investigate that as well. I want to know who is responsible."

"I'll turn this place inside out," Smalls said.

Jackson turned back to Franklin. "Don't tell me we're back to square one."

"We can still piece together the material the programmers haven't deleted off their machines and knit it together with the good parts of the copy."

Jackson put his glasses back on and looked sharply at Franklin. "Lilypad was still on the programmer machines?"

"Backed up to the other servers. They're supposed to clean up what they've been working on, but I'm not strict about it until the product is in the bag, so there are bits and pieces here and there. The upside is we're not starting from scratch, but it's still a major undertaking. It's hard to guess at this point, Stuart. Six months, maybe. I'll know better after we get started."

Jackson shook his head. "Six months? This company is bleeding cash right now. We've got to do everything we can to support the stock price. Lilypad 5 was all we had between us and the wall. We've got to get it out as quickly as possible." He turned to Smalls. "Leroy, can you get the fire restoration people in here tomorrow?"

Smalls nodded. "Consider it done."

"Good. Ronnie, order in any new equipment we need. Expedite it. Commandeer any useful equipment we already have."

"What about our other projects?"

"None of our other projects will roll out in time to save the company, so we can put them on hold if we have to. On Monday, I want anyone who can help with Lilypad working full time on this project. And Ronnie, find an office for me. I'm going to work out of this location until I'm satisfied things are back on track." He looked from Franklin to Smalls and back. "We have to keep this fiasco quiet, play down the extent of the damage; we want the press to think this fire is a minor setback that's well under control. I'll massage the board of directors. We've got to do everything we can to push Lilypad out the door. Once it's out, we'll all be in the clear."

4: The Handoff

The next morning, Saturday, Franklin stood in his kitchen at the brown granite island counter eating a toasted bagel slathered with butter and reading the *Cloverdale Gazette*. His coffee was lukewarm. Melanie stood with her back to him at the sink, rinsing dishes to go into the dishwasher and keeping an eye on the birdfeeder on the steel post in the side yard. She was still in her robe and slippers, but she'd already put on her makeup. She turned off the water and dried her hands. "Looks like we got a little more snow last night. Was that after you got back?"

Franklin looked up from the sports section to meet her eyes. "I'm sorry. Did I wake you going out? I got a call from Smalls. There was a fire at the office."

"A fire?"

"Yeah. Burned up a server on the fourth floor. What a mess. Firemen and the whole works. Stuart was there as well." He pushed the metro section across to her and pointed at the article.

Melanie squinted to read the headline. "But no one was hurt?"

"No. The building was empty except for the security guard who called it in." He slurped his coffee. "The main problem is computer damage. The new product we thought we were rolling out next month? Now it's six months of hard work away."

"So, what does that mean for us?"

"It means the bonus and the opportunity to sell stock also moved six months."

"So my new car lease and Kat's birthday?"

"We have to stay on our budget for the next six months."

"She's going to be crushed."

"I know. It's got me thinking about my time at Leapfrog. The place just isn't on the move anymore. I'm beginning to think it's run its course; that I should find a new job before the place goes under and everyone associated with it is tainted. And a signing bonus would take care of Kat's birthday. She could have whatever car she wanted — within reason."

"And that's the only way?"

"I'm not promising anything. I haven't looked into any opportunities, but yeah, if we want any extra cash in the next six months, that's it."

Melanie stood with her hands on her hips, a carefully neutral expression on her face. "Next year is Kat's senior year of high school. She's first chair flute in the orchestra and she's going to be captain of the dance team. There's no way we can move until after graduation, so you'll have to think of some other way." She looked up at the wall clock. "My goodness, I've got to get dressed. Jody will be along any minute."

"Busy morning?"

"We're going to get coffee and do a little shopping. Kat will be back from practice in an hour. You should take her to lunch."

He nodded.

"A little father-daughter time might spur your imagination." She kissed his cheek and headed for the upstairs.

He watched her walk away. Was there any idea for making her happy that she wouldn't shoot down? What was he supposed to do, bend over and pull the money out of his ass? In the world according to Melanie, there was no problem that couldn't be solved by restaurant food and some light shopping. Christ. He picked up the sports section and tried to go back to the article he was reading, but he just couldn't focus. He glanced down at the front page of Metro. Well, at least the first part of the plan had been successful. The computer was wrecked. They'd bought an extra six months to find and fix the problems in Lilypad. So maybe his luck was changing. All Samantha had to do now was palm off the bad program and get rid of the thieves.

At 11:00 a.m., Samantha sat with Tess and Joe at the far end of the food court of the old Lakeview Mall on the northeast side of Cloverdale. The food court was the usual assortment of coffee, sub, burger, pizza, Tex-Mex, and Chinese fast food restaurants surrounding a shared seating area located next to the public restrooms and a stairwell and across from the six-plex second-run movie theater. There were a few teenagers goofing near the Borderlands Tacos and a couple of moms with small children seated at the tables. Samantha was nursing a thin, flat-tasting cappuccino. The tablet computer that contained the bad version of Lilypad 5 sat in a Victoria's Secret bag under some pink tissue on the table in front of her. Tess sat across from her. She'd taken off her black wool coat and hung it over the back of her seat. A bottle of water sat on the table in front of her. Joe sat to Samantha's right and Tess's left. His right hand was in the pocket of his brown leather jacket and his left hand lay on the table as if he were planning on picking something up.

"The clock is ticking," Joe said. "He's got fifteen minutes."

"He'll be here," Samantha said.

"I hope so." He glanced slowly to his left.

Tess reached over and patted Samantha's hand. She smiled. "Which way you going to run if the cops come?"

"Which way?"

"Yeah," Tess continued. "Which way? Everyone goes a different way; we meet up later. I like to do it quiet, so I'm running for the J.C. Penney, lose them in there, go out one of the outside doors."

Joe grinned. "I'm going loud. Emergency exit next to the restrooms. The alarms go off and all hell breaks loose." He looked at Samantha. "Don't go to your own car. Come back later for your vehicle. Don't run toward a location you have in mind. Just keep moving away from the trouble."

Samantha tapped the side of the Victoria's Secret bag. "This is just to pass the time, scare the greenhorn, isn't it?"

Tess twisted the cap down on her water. "Hope so."

Samantha looked past Tess. "There he is."

A tall, thin man in his mid-twenties with short red hair and pasty, freckled skin, wearing black jeans, a black, long-sleeve t-shirt, and an open black overcoat, came into the food court from the mall and walked up to the table. He was carrying a soft black satchel over his shoulder. He looked around as if he were expecting the police to jump up from the nearby tables. "Hello, Samantha."

"Hi, Fred."

"You got my gift?"

"Right here." She pointed to the Victoria's Secret bag.

He peeked in the top.

Joe motioned with his head. "Have a seat."

Olsen slipped the satchel off his shoulder and set it down next to Samantha. "I don't think so."

Samantha unzipped the satchel. She saw a packet of bills with a one hundred dollar bill on top. She smiled.

"Good luck." Olsen picked up the Victoria's Secret bag and walked away, weaving through the tables toward the stairwell.

Samantha, Joe, and Tess all stood up. Samantha put the satchel on the table, reached in, and thumbed through the money. Her mouth fell open. "We've been ripped off. It's mostly paper."

They rushed after Olsen, who was now most of the way through the seating area. They dodged through the tables, hoping to get within distance of catching him before he looked back. Joe almost knocked down a mom carrying a tray of burgers and soft drinks for three grade-schoolers. "Hey," she yelled, "watch where you're going."

Olsen looked over his shoulder just before he opened the stairwell door, threw his weight against the steel door, and started to run. Samantha reached the door just as it clicked shut, pushed on the bar, threw it wide open, crossed the landing in two steps, the black satchel swinging by its shoulder strap from her hand, and went down the first two steps all at once. The satchel swung under her snow boot, the strap tangling around her leg. She fell down the rest of the steps to the landing between the floors, rolling hard, trying to protect her head with her arms, and landed on her right leg with a sickening crack. Joe and Tess were right behind her, but now she blocked the way. They heard a stairwell door open and shut below them.

"Goddamn idiot." Joe kicked the air. "He thinks we won't kill him over the money."

Tess knelt beside Samantha. "Don't get up."

Samantha grimaced. "My leg."

Joe stood over her. The lower part of her right leg was bent at an unnatural angle. "Leg's broken, honey. That was a hell of a fall. Lucky you didn't snap your neck."

Tess patted Samantha's cheek. "Your pupils look okay. Does it hurt when you breathe?"

"No."

"Where's your phone?"

"In my coat pocket."

Tess fished Samantha's phone out of her pocket and dialed 911. She tried to imitate Samantha's voice. "I'm at Lakeview Mall. I fell down the stairwell by the food court. I can't move. I can't stay awake." She hung up and handed the phone back to Samantha. "You'll be okay. Help is on the way."

"Don't leave me here."

Tess stroked Samantha's hair. "Have to. Can't be seen here with you. Raises too many questions."

Joe squatted next to her. "Pay attention. This is your story. You lost track of time. Got in a hurry. That's why you were running. You slipped and lost your balance. Say it."

She said it.

"Stick with it. It doesn't sound believable now, but as long as you stick with it, it will do. We'll be in touch about our money."

Tess picked up the satchel. "I'll get this out of the way."

They stepped over her and disappeared down the stairwell. Samantha lay there, gritting her teeth, trying to control her breathing, tears welling up in her eyes until they overflowed the sockets and ran down her cheeks. She'd read somewhere that thinking about something else could help lessen the pain, but all she could think about was how close she was to being found out, fired, and jailed. And those thoughts only made her leg hurt worse. She'd dug herself into a hole. She should have taken her chances with telling Jackson the truth about the Lilypad project. He might have only fired Ronnie. Instead, she'd let Ronnie talk her into this crazy plan, a plan that got her no closer to keeping her job, a plan where she now had multiple lies and liars to keep track of.

Why had Ronnie insisted on selling the buggy program to Olsen? There was some sort of bad blood between them, but it was a risk she and Ronnie hadn't needed to take. But she had agreed to do it so that Ronnie wouldn't have to scrounge up another $50,000. Now Olsen had double-crossed them. What would he do when he discovered that Lilypad was junk? Blackmail her? She wiped her eyes with her sleeve. What were Joe and Tess going to do now? The money was gone. And Ronnie's only connection to this stupidity was her. He could toss her under the bus at will. God, she was a fool. She held up her phone and looked at the time. She felt dizzy. The pounding in her leg seemed to reverberate through her body. The last thing she remembered was the phone falling on her chest.

When she woke up, someone was shining a light in her eye. "Ms. Bartel, Ms. Bartel, can you hear me?"

"Yes."

"You're in the emergency room. You had an accident."

"I remember." She was lying on her back. Something was wrapped around her neck. As her eyes came into focus, she saw an African-American woman in blue scrubs, her black hair tied back and covered with a cap, leaning over her, a stethoscope hanging from her neck.

"Your leg is broken. You may have a concussion. I'm going to give you something for the pain; then you're going to x-ray."

"Okay."

"I'm Dr. Philips. Don't worry. We're going to take good care of you."

The doctor's face disappeared. Another woman's face appeared. She had gray-streaked light brown hair and a bright smile. "I'm going to give you a shot." Samantha knew, somehow, that she'd been given a shot in the hip, but she didn't feel it. "Is there someone we can call? Your husband? "

"My nephew. Number's in my phone. Brandon Bartel."

"We've got it. Relax, hon. We're going for a ride."

Leroy Smalls rapped his knuckles on the open door to Samantha's room at Mercy Medical Center and stepped in. Samantha was lying in bed watching a cooking show on the TV that hung from the ceiling across from the bed. Her casted right leg peeked out from under the thin white cotton blanket that covered her up to her arms. The room was small, but cheerful. There were monitors arrayed on her right, but they didn't seem to be turned on. On her left, two metal-framed, vinyl-cushioned chairs crowded the space between the bed and the windows, which looked out on two leafless oak trees and a picnic table covered in snow.

"Leroy," she said, "how did you find me here?"

"I don't think I'd keep my job very long if I couldn't find a member of our management team." He looked her over. "How are you doing?"

"I'm doing okay. Broken leg, bruises; they're keeping me overnight for observation. I'm feeling pretty foolish. Tripping over my own feet and falling down the stairs? From now on I'm getting all my exercise at the fitness center."

"Can I talk with you a few minutes? Are you up to it?"

"Sure. What's on your mind?" She turned off the TV.

Smalls shuffled into the space between the bed and the chairs and sat in the chair nearest Samantha's head. "You heard about the fire?"

"Yeah, Ronnie called me. New project all screwed up. We're supposed to be hard at it on Monday. Now I don't know if I'll be there."

"Have you noticed anything at the office that maybe didn't attract your attention before but since the fire would seem—how to put it—peculiar?"

"I thought the fire was an accident."

"That's what the fire department says. I'm just going over the lay of the land, earning my pay."

Samantha nodded. "It was just the usual insanity that accompanies the countdown to a new product rollout."

"Ronnie seem good to you?"

"Ronnie?"

"He doesn't seem stressed-out, anxious, like he's acting like himself instead of being himself?"

"Gosh, Leroy, I haven't really noticed anything. But I haven't been paying that much attention."

"What about that intern?"

"Tess?"

"Yeah, Tess. I'll want to talk with her."

"Her address and phone number are in the office. I'm sure Carol can get them for you."

Smalls gripped the arms of his chair and pushed himself up. "Well, I've been here long enough. Get some rest. If you think of anything else —"

"I'll let you know. It would just be crazy if somebody did this on purpose. Who knows what they might do next?"

"I wouldn't worry too much. The fire department is probably right."

Samantha turned the TV back on.

Smalls walked down the hall to the elevator. The fire was surely an accident. There was no evidence to the contrary. But why did he have the feeling that Ronnie and Samantha were hiding something? He didn't think Sam was lying, but something just wasn't right. And then there were the problems with the security cameras that Gregory had noted in the logs. That and the scrambled recording. He punched the down button on the elevator. He'd just have to keep picking at this puzzle until he figured it out.

After dinner, Samantha lay in her hospital bed thumbing through a *Kiplinger's Personal Finance* when there was a knock on the open door. She turned her head. Franklin sauntered into her room. He held a glass vase of mixed red and yellow carnations out away from himself as if he were afraid of spilling water on his olive colored parka.

Samantha smiled. "You get those in the lobby?"

"Touché." He set the vase on a counter near her head.

"Well, they are pretty. Thanks."

"Looks like you got banged up pretty well. That sure takes the suspicion off you. Wish I had thought of it."

"Oh, yeah, I'm the master planner. Threw myself down the stairs." She adjusted her cotton blanket. "But you didn't come by to comment on my injuries; what's on your mind?"

Franklin started to speak, glanced over his shoulder, shut the door to the room, and than came up close to her bed. "Outside of your accident, everything looks good. Stuart bought the story. We've got six months. All the damage was contained in the one server. All we have to do is pull together the pieces off the programmers' machines, figure out where the glitches are, and reassemble the new, improved Lilypad 5."

"Wonderful. Olsen ripped us off. That's how I broke my leg."

"But he got the messed-up version?"

"Yeah."

"And you added a virus to contaminate whatever machine he puts it on?"

"Did that Friday before I left work."

"Good. He'll get what he deserves." Franklin put his hands in his pockets.

"What about the thieves?" Samantha asked. "I haven't heard from them since the mall."

"Maybe they ran; I don't know. Just let me know if they get in contact with you. That was fifty thousand well spent."

"What account did you take the money from?"

"I'm not that big a fool, Sam. You can't mess with the books. I used my own money."

"Smalls came by to see me this afternoon."

"Stuart's got him sniffing around, but there's nothing for him to find. You going to be in the office on Monday?"

"That's my plan."

"Well, rest up. Good thing you've got that intern to help you while you're hobbling around. If you need anything, call my personal number."

Samantha watched him leave. She picked up her magazine. Fifty thousand dollars of his own money. That was bullshit. Ronnie wouldn't buy a client a cup of coffee without filing an expense report. The cheapest secret Santa gifts were always his. There was no way he put that money up. He got it from somewhere. She just hoped that somewhere didn't blow up in their faces until after Lilypad was fixed.

When Brandon walked into the Silver Moose Tavern, he stood inside the door to get his bearings. He'd never been there before. Never even been out of a moving car in this neighborhood before. A large, oval dark-stained bar dominated the center of the room. Matching booths lined both walls. At the back were the bathrooms and the door to the parking lot. Knots of men in work clothes and ball caps stood at the bar, some with their coats on. Mixed groups of men and women sat at the booths with pitchers of beer in front of them, talking in low voices and laughing out loud. The bartender, a large, gray-haired man wearing a blue plaid flannel shirt with the sleeves rolled up, sized Brandon up with a scowl. Brandon started walking toward the back, glancing in the booths, looking for the man he'd come here to see. He found him sitting alone in the back corner booth. Jonny Chaos was squat and fat. Stringy black hair hung down in his eyes and he wore heavy rings on all the fingers of his hands. Two tattooed thugs wearing brown canvas work coats stood at the bar nearby. Brandon kept his hands in the pockets of his leather coat. "Hey, Jonny."

The closest thug started toward him, shaved head, neck tattoos and empty eyes, but Jonny waved him off. "It's okay, Bobby." The thug stepped back to the bar.

Jonny looked at Brandon. "What kept you?"

Brandon shrugged. "Never been here before."

"Sit down."

Brandon sat in the booth. Jonny looked him over. "Haven't heard from you in a long time, not since you did that little piece of hacking for me."

"But that worked out for you, didn't it?"

"No complaints." Jonny rubbed his hands together. "So now you want to sell me something. You sure it works?"

"Absolutely. You can use it to mine credit card numbers, names, zip codes, and other kinds of useful intelligence. Your guy goes to a website where they store credit information, he plugs in this program, and boom, you've got the info."

"You sure? 'Cause thirty thousand is real American money."

"It works."

"If it turns out it's sugar pills and not Viagra, you will definitely live long enough to regret your mistake. You understand what I mean?"

"This is the real thing."

Jonny picked up a brown paper sack off the seat beside him and set it on the table. Brandon took his hand out of his pocket and put the thumb drive on the table. Jonny took the thumb drive. Brandon took the paper sack and shoved it inside his coat.

Jonny smiled. "Aren't you going to count it?"

Brandon stuck out his hand. "Great doing business with you."

Jonny ignored the hand. Brandon slid out of the booth and walked back toward the front door. He could feel everyone's eyes on him, sizing him up, wondering what his business was with a criminal like Jonny Chaos. He pushed the door open and went back out into the freezing night. Either way he looked, all he could see were boarded-up storefronts mixed with run-down, four-story walk-up apartment buildings. Across the street, somebody was lying in a doorway bundled up in rags. Brandon's Civic was halfway down the block. At least it was on this side of the street. He started toward it, thought he heard something behind him, and looked back. Nothing. He turned back toward his car. Bobby, the thug with the shaved head, was standing in front of him, his hands in his canvas coat pockets, his chin tucked down against the cold. Brandon took a step back. Bobby grinned, showing a silver tooth. "No worries, Junior. Chaos wanted to make sure you got to your car all right. Just part of the service."

Brandon hurried down the street to the Civic, the hulking thug in his wake. As he opened the car door, Bobby turned his back. "Thanks," Brandon said.

Bobby spoke over his shoulder. "Don't thank me. I'd have robbed you and left you in the street. Have a nice day."

Brandon got in the car, locked the doors, and started the engine. Then he took the paper sack out of his coat. It was all there: $30,000. He grinned. Good thing he'd made a copy of Lilypad. Aunt Samantha had gotten stiffed by Olsen, so there was no way she could pay him what she promised. It was still hard to believe that she would do anything dishonest. It had seemed like a bizarre dream when she'd first asked him to help her steal the program. She must be in a pretty tight spot. But that wasn't his problem. He'd gotten himself paid. Now he had enough money to pay off his school loans and make something of his life. The world was opening up in front of him. He shoved the sack back into his coat. This neighborhood was shit. He didn't even feel safe locked in his car. He glanced into his rearview mirror and pulled away from the curb.

It was after 9:00 p.m. by the time Franklin knocked on the door of his girlfriend Angie's apartment. She lived at the Ridgeview Apartments, a collection of stuccoed and red tile roofed apartments directly across the street from the entrance to the Cloverdale Golf and Country Club, where Franklin was a member and where she worked as a personal trainer and yoga instructor. Angie was thirty-two years old, tall, blue-eyed, and blonde. She had a rower's hard shoulders and a schoolgirl's slim hips. She answered the door wearing black yoga pants and a scoop-necked baby blue long-sleeve t-shirt that exposed a lot of cleavage. "What a surprise," she said. "Come on in."

He kissed her and she stepped back to let him into the room. "I thought Saturdays you took Melanie out."

"Girls' night out." He slipped out of his parka. "I can't stay, though. She'll be home soon."

"So why did you stop by?"

"I just had to see you, touch your hand, even if only for a minute."

She didn't reply. She just stood there, hands on hips, and rolled her eyes.

He shook the brown paper bag he held in his hand. "I need to make a deposit."

Angie's apartment was an open-floor-plan one bedroom with neutral tan wall-to-wall carpeting. A white leather sofa sat perpendicular to the windows and faced a forty-two inch TV, which sat below a set of simple white shelves decorated with small glass figurines and hand-thrown clay pots glazed in primary colors. Beyond the sofa was a square, glass-topped table, which butted up against the counter that separated the galley kitchen from the rest of the room. Franklin walked back through the living room into her bedroom, flipped the light switch, opened her walk-in closet, and knelt down in front of the safe he'd had installed there.

Angie stood behind him. "I don't know why I put up with you."

"Me neither. Guess I'll have to do until someone better comes along—someone younger, better looking, richer."

He opened the safe, took a rubber-banded bundle of cash out of the paper bag, and laid the bundle on top of the money that was already in the safe. Then he shut the door and spun the dial. "That's done."

They went back out to the living room. Franklin shoved the empty bag into the pocket of his parka. "Actually, I was surprised to find you here."

"Where else would I be?" she said.

"It's Saturday night."

"Why's Melanie out with her girlfriends?"

"I wasn't paying much attention. Somebody's getting divorced or something. Needs the collective wisdom of the harpies." He shrugged. "Really? I don't know. She said it was 'ladies assemble' and I said 'okay.'"

"You got time for a drink?"

He glanced at his wristwatch. "One glass of wine."

He followed her into the kitchen area. She poured two glasses of merlot from an opened bottle on the counter. "Thanks." He took a sip, looked at the way she was holding her glass, and said, "What's on your mind?"

"I'm not trying to pressure you, but I was just wondering where all this is going." She gestured around the room with her free hand. "I mean, it's Saturday night, you're here—I don't think you're checking up on me—the amount of time we've been together, most guys would be leaving a few clothes and a toothbrush, but you leave a safe in the bedroom closet."

"So why am I hiding money here instead of just opening a bank account or safety deposit box?"

She nodded.

"Let's sit down." She followed him to the sofa. He put his half-empty wine glass down on the glass-topped coffee table. "So what do you think is going on?"

"I don't know. I don't think it's dirty money. You're a regular guy with a fulltime job. You belong to the golf and country club. All the people I've seen you with are tech types or managers."

He took her hand in his, but he looked at the figurines on the shelves directly above the TV. "I don't want my wife to find out about this money. More importantly, I don't want Melanie's lawyer to find out about this money."

"Melanie's lawyer?"

"Kat will graduate next year. Then she's off to college. Once she's gone, I'm going to divorce Melanie. We just don't have anything in common anymore. It's sad to say, but that's the way it is. And Melanie likes her money. She'll try to take me to the cleaners for sure. Whatever is in the accounts, she'll get half of. So right now I'm trying to sock back as much money as I can out of sight."

"You're going to divorce Melanie?"

"That's right."

Angie gulped down the rest of her wine and set her glass on the coffee table. "And you're stashing your money in a safe at my house for the next year, year and a half?"

He nodded.

"Then what?"

He looked down at the sofa cushion between them. "I know I'm a little old for you, that we've just been fooling around here until you find the right guy —"

"It's not like that."

"But I was hoping you might marry me."

"Oh, Ronnie." She threw her arms around him. "You don't know how much I've been wanting to hear you say that."

"Really? I was afraid you'd say 'no.'" He kissed her. Then he glanced at his wristwatch. "I hate to say this, but I've got to go."

"Can't you stay just a little while?"

He shook his head. "We have to be smart. I don't want Melanie to suspect anything. I know it seems like a long time to Kat's graduation now, but it'll be here before you know it. And then we'll be together always, every day."

He got up and put on his parka. She kissed him again. "Call me," she said.

"As soon as I can." He went out to his Volvo in the parking lot. A hard frost was starting to form on the windshield. He started the car, and then scraped the frost off the windshield while the car warmed up. The cold night air was sharp and invigorating. He felt great. He tossed the ice scraper into the back seat as he climbed back into the front. He would definitely be home before Melanie. She wasn't going to suspect a thing. And now he had Angie wrapped around his finger. With marriage just over the horizon, she'd do whatever he asked. And who knew? He might actually marry her if he had nothing better to do.

Samantha turned off the TV and set the remote on the counter by her head. She glanced toward the bathroom door, thought about how hard it was to get out of bed and hobble over to the toilet, and decided that she really didn't need to go to the bathroom before she fell asleep. The hospital was amazingly quiet — quieter than her condo. It gave her the willies. But tomorrow she'd be out of here; she'd spend the day on the sofa watching DVDs. Monday would be the real test, sitting in the office as if she knew nothing, the clock ticking on rebuilding Lilypad. They had to make it work. Their jobs and their retirements were on the line. Monday. She started to drift off when she realized someone was in her room. She opened her eyes. Joe and Tess were standing over her bed, wolfish eyes set in confident faces. Tess smiled a big, beautiful movie-star smile. "What's happening, boss?"

Samantha reached for the controller to raise the head of the bed.

Joe gave her a sympathetic look. "Let me help, Samantha." He pushed the button on the controller. Her head came up. "How's that?"

She looked from one to the other; they were still dressed as they had been at the mall, Tess in her black wool coat, Joe in his brown leather jacket. Then she looked to make sure her assistance button was clipped to the edge of her bed in easy reach. "Why are you here?"

"Did we wake you, honey?" Tess said. "We tried to get here earlier, but you seemed to have a cascade of visitors."

"You're a popular girl," Joe said. "I hope you had your story straight."

Samantha nodded. "You wouldn't believe what a klutz I am. But it's not as bad as it looks. I'm just here overnight for observation."

Tess patted her hand. "That's wonderful."

"After the fiasco at the mall, I'm kind of surprised to see you."

"I don't know why," Joe said. "You owe us fifty thousand, so we're on you like white on rice."

"I gave you the fifty thousand ahead. I was supposed to give you the other fifty after I collected. I didn't collect. You were there. You saw what happened."

Joe sighed. "Exactly. But did we see you get ripped off or did we see you play out a scam to rip us off?"

"My leg got broken."

"Accidents happen in the best laid plans."

"Smalls was here asking questions about the fire."

Joe shrugged. "And that's supposed to scare us? Of course he's going to ask questions. That's his job. And the longer we're around, the more suspicious he's going to become."

Tess rubbed Joe's arm. "Don't get testy, baby. Sam's going to do everything she can to help us. Aren't you, Sam?"

"I don't know what I can do."

Joe stepped toward her. "If we don't get paid, we're going to expose you."

"How is that going to help you?"

"Focus your mind," Joe said. He tapped a finger against his forehead. "Arguing won't get you out of this."

"Okay, okay," Samantha said. "How much money was in the bag Olsen left?"

"One thousand."

"That bastard. So I still owe forty-nine."

Joe nodded. "We've been using our time, but we'll accept that."

"So where do you think it's going to come from?"

"Squeeze it out of your nephew. I don't care."

"Baby," Tess said to Joe, "you know we talked about this. You need to be positive. Take a deep breath." She turned to Samantha. "Tell us about Olsen. You don't care what happens to him, do you?"

She rapped on her leg cast with her knuckles. "I've got six weeks not to care about him. Fred Olsen is a third-rate tech geek. He owns Paramount Design. He has trouble playing with others, so he's mainly a one-man shop plus temporaries. He thinks he's the genius that's hiding in plain sight, but he can't design anything really original, so he buys other people's ideas and claims he came up with them. That's why he was the perfect person to sell the program to."

Tess nodded. "But he must have been short on cash."

"Or he thought he didn't have to pay because I wouldn't be able to complain if he ripped me off."

Tess glanced at Joe. He shook his head as if he had nothing else to say. She turned back to Samantha. "I've got confidence in you. Keep working this problem and you'll find the money to pay us." She bent down and kissed Samantha on the lips. Then she and Joe left the room.

Samantha lay in bed, staring at the wall. What had she expected? Of course they would squeeze her. They were crooks. They wanted their money. Blackmailing her was easier than moving on to steal from someone else. They knew about her and Brandon, and they knew that Olsen had the program. What was the worst that could happen if she were exposed? She wasn't at the office on the night of the fire. Olsen would deny. Brandon would deny. Jackson would fire her if he believed she sold Lilypad, but she was going to be fired anyway if they didn't find a way to fix it. Either way, she wouldn't be able to get another job.

The real problem was the stock price. If the stock tanked, she was screwed. She had to stay on the job, had to fix Lilypad. If she were fired, and then sold her stock, and Lilypad tanked, Jackson would surely report her for insider trading. Even if she didn't go to jail, fines and lawyers would eat up her money. They had to find a way to fix Lilypad. Then she could keep her job and sell her stock when the price shot up. Her retirement would be secure. She picked up her cell phone off the counter by her head. "Ronnie? This is Samantha."

"Jesus, Sam, it's kind of late. You okay?"

"The thieves were just here to see me."

"Don't use the 'T' word."

"They want the rest of their — uh — potatoes."

"Potatoes? Okay. They shouldn't have let the potato man get away from the farmer's market."

"Yeah, well, they don't care. They still want the second bag. Are you going to help or not?"

"I'm not digging up any more potatoes. I've already done my part and they don't know who I am."

"You're not going to help?"

"It's your turn to dig up the potatoes if there aren't enough."

"But that's your area of expertise."

"Not anymore. We're on to the next phase as far as I'm concerned. You're a big girl, Sam. Figure it out. Anything else I can help you with?" The line was silent for a moment. "No? Well, I'll see you Monday."

Samantha looked at her phone. It was the typical Ronnie Franklin move and she hadn't seen it coming. Why should he supply any more money? He was completely in the clear. There was nothing to tie him to the fire. She'd contacted the thieves; she'd brought in her nephew; she was at the meeting with Olsen. She couldn't pressure Ronnie for the money without exposing herself. And once she was exposed, she'd just look like she was trying to spread the blame if she accused him.

Why, why, why did she always have to be the team player? That's the way Ronnie always wormed her into one of his schemes. And now he was going to leave her holding the bag. She blew her nose. She didn't have $50,000 in cash. She didn't control any budget line with anywhere near that amount of loose money in it. Besides, if she used company money, she'd have to account for it. And there was no way she could raise $50,000 on her own, short of borrowing against her condo. The condo was all she had. There was no way she was going to take out a mortgage. She was going to have to stall, and keep stalling, until she could figure some way to get rid of the thieves.

Joe looked into the living room at Tess. "You want a drink?" He was standing at the almond Formica counter of the kitchenette in the rundown furnished apartment they rented by the week.

Tess looked up at him from the black leather sofa. "Make it two fingers, baby."

Joe poured Irish whiskey into two water glasses and carried them into the living room. He handed one to Tess, sat down next to her, kicked off his hiking boots, and put his stocking feet up on the dark oak coffee table. "What a day." He took a drink.

Tess twined her legs with his and leaned against his shoulder. "I didn't expect that kid—what's his name? Olsen—to run at the mall."

"Me neither. It was so obvious I couldn't even believe it was happening for a second there."

"You believe her? Samantha, I mean; you believe she got ripped off?" Tess asked.

"Don't know. She's lying about something, though. You think I pushed her hard enough?"

"I think she got the message. How hard can you push in a hospital room?"

He nodded thoughtfully.

Tess continued. "Is the well tapped out?"

Joe shook his head. He put his arm around her. "There's more than fifty thousand lying around here. Let's start shaking the trees and see what falls out. We've got Samantha and Brandon standing between us and any trouble. If they come under too much pressure, we can always run."

"What you got in mind?"

"Keep working the office. What about this Franklin guy? He's her boss, right?"

"He's a randy old bastard."

"Check him out. Maybe he's crooked, too. And the nephew. He doesn't smell or have head lice, does he? Work on him a little. Might be something there."

She drank from her glass and then rested her head on his chest. "You're going to pick at this deal until you find me a challenge."

He gave her a squeeze. "That's not a problem for you, is it? You're not having second thoughts?"

"I'm fine with it, baby. I don't have PTSD. I'm completely over what happened in Seanboro. I'm my old self. I'm good to go. Brandon may be a little young for me to work, but I'll get him figured out if that's what it takes."

"That's the spirit."

"What are you going to do while I'm digging up office dirt?"

"I'm going to check into this Olsen guy. He owes us some money. Plus he hurt my feelings."

"Ouch."

He cradled her head in his arms to kiss her and then took another sip of whiskey. "Thus far, I haven't heard a single name that scares me. They're all amateurs and they're all crooked. There's got to be some more low-hanging fruit around here somewhere."

She set her glass on the coffee table. "You're a bad, bad boy."

He looked into her laughing eyes. She did have her confidence back. She was strong and tough and capable of seducing any man who fell in their path. "There's always room for improvement."

She slipped her hand under his t-shirt, stroked his chest, and then kissed him on the lips. He set his drink down, put his arms around her, and eased her down onto the sofa. "What would I do without you?" he whispered.

She smiled and murmured, "I'm sure you'd think of something."

5: Cards on the Table

Sunday morning at 11:00 a.m., Brandon held Samantha by the arm as they climbed up the three concrete steps to the front porch of her one-story condo. Samantha was on crutches. She wore her down coat over her pink-striped nightgown. On her good leg, she wore a winter boot. On her casted leg, a green hiking sock covered her toes. "Hold on tight," she said. She shoved her key into the lock and Brandon turned the handle.

"Okay," Brandon said, "only a few more steps." He helped her hobble over to the blue corduroy sofa in front of the big screen TV, tugged her coat off onto the hardwood floor, took the crutches and eased her down into a sitting position.

"I need to lose some weight," she said.

"Plenty of time for that. Right now you need to concentrate on your leg." He picked up her coat, closed the front door, and hung the coat up in the front closet. "Okay." He dragged over a leather cube footstool for her to put her feet up on. "You all right for now? I'll go get your bag."

"Give me that throw first." She pointed at a red fleece throw on the back of the side chair.

He shook it open and laid it over her legs. She pulled it up to her middle. "Okay," she said, "I'm good."

Brandon went back out to his car, which was parked in her driveway, and brought in her overnight bag. "I'll put this in your bedroom."

"Great."

He said something from the bedroom, but she couldn't hear him. When she could see him, she said, "What did you say?"

"You going to be all right by yourself? You're not moving around so well."

"I'll be fine as soon as I get the hang of things. I've got microwave dinners and breakfast cereal. And," she held up her cell phone, "delivery pizza, Chinese, vegetarian. Just get me settled. If I get in bad trouble, I'll give you a call. You don't want to hang around here."

"Okay." He went into the kitchen and got three bottles of water, a bag of peeled baby carrots, some celery sticks, and a small container of vanilla yogurt out of the refrigerator. He arranged them on a tray before he carried them in to her and set them on the sofa beside her.

"Guess I'm going to have to learn to use the crutches if I don't want to starve to death."

He smiled. "Aunt Sam, you want me to bring you a bucket to pee in?"

"Ha, ha, ha," she said. "Why don't you hand me one of those crutches so I can smack you with it."

He sat down on the other side of the tray. "I think you're going to be all right."

She fished a carrot out of the bag. "That's what I keep telling you." Her eyebrows went up. "Wait a minute. You never call me 'Aunt Sam' anymore. What's up?"

"You remember Jesse and Bill?"

"Your college buddies."

"They're pulling together an animation startup out in San Francisco. They've asked me to come work with them, so I'm giving notice at Leapfrog."

She reached over and patted his hand. "Good for you."

"I just didn't want you to think I didn't appreciate your help getting me a job at Leapfrog after I graduated."

She waved it off. "Don't give it any thought. You deserve an opportunity like this. I hope you kids design some excellent products and make a pile of money."

"Thanks. One other thing. I can understand if you don't want to talk about this right now, but what are you going to do about Olsen?"

"You mean the money? Fair question." She ate another carrot. "I'm not exactly sure what to do. We don't have any leverage. He stole what we stole. I'm not going to shoot him." She frowned. "I'm sorry I can't pay you what I promised." She picked up a celery stick, and then she started laughing, holding the celery in her hand and laughing until the tears started.

"Samantha," Brandon said. "Samantha, what's so funny?"

She wiped her face on her sleeve. "The fall down the stairs must have knocked more loose than I thought. I'd forgotten for a minute there that I'd put a virus in Lilypad. It could take a few days, but then Olsen's computers will be all screwed up." She chuckled. "He's going to be pissed. Serves him right. Besides—I probably shouldn't tell you this—Lilypad is a dog. It wasn't ready to roll out. The fire was the only way we could think of to get more time to work on it without losing our jobs." She looked him in the eye. "If we can't fix it, the company will probably go bankrupt. So you're getting out at the best time possible. If you can keep your luck, you'll end up a billionaire."

Brandon's mouth was hanging open. "Lilypad is crap and you loaded it with what? A worm? A Trojan horse?"

Samantha smiled. "Just a simple virus. I didn't have time to get fancy. It should raise havoc with his network, though, particularly if it gets into his wireless router." She dipped the celery stick in the yogurt and put it in her mouth. "Life would be wonderful if I wasn't afraid of being fired in the next six months."

"I'm sure you'll fix Lilypad." Brandon made a show of looking at his watch. "So are you all set? I've got to get going."

"Hand me the TV remote."

He got the remote off the table under the big screen TV and handed it to her. "Call me if you need anything." He started toward the door.

"Hey, could you take a cab out to the mall and drive my car back? Keys are in my coat."

"Yeah, sure. Later today, okay?"

"I'm not going anywhere."

He opened the coat closet and fished her keys out of her coat. "Want me to take them off the ring?"

"Leave them together."

"Okay."

"Thanks, Brandon. You're a gem."

Brandon sat in his car with the engine turned on. He banged his fists against the steering wheel. Fuck, fuck, fuck, fuck. He got out his phone and called Jonny Chaos. No answer. Where was Chaos's office? In old town, across the bridge — no, he moved to that old storefront on Vine. Brandon pulled away from the curb. He had to warn Chaos before he tried to use the program. Chaos had the thumb drive — what? Sixteen hours. It was Sunday. The thumb drive could be sitting on a desk. Hell, it could still be in Chaos's pocket. He could have given it to one of his guys. That guy could have gotten loaded, still be sleeping it off. Brandon turned onto Seventh Street. He tried Chaos's phone number again. "Yeah?"

"Chaos? This is Brandon. Don't use the thumb drive. It's screwed up."

Chaos sighed. "A little late for that."

"I'm on my way. I'll fix your computers; give you your money back."

"That's a great offer, kid. What did I tell you last night? Do you remember? Turns out it's not Viagra. It's not even sugar pills; it's rat poison."

"Hey, I was screwed, too."

"Not my problem."

"I'll make this right."

"I'm sure you will. Lucky for you the computer we plugged it into didn't matter. You're going to give me back my thirty thousand, plus another fifteen for my trouble. The quicker you do it, the more likely you won't be doing it from a hospital bed. Enjoy the day."

Brandon tossed his phone into the front passenger's seat. Shit. He didn't have $15,000. Since he started at Leapfrog three years ago, he'd been using most of his salary to pay down his college loans. Chaos's $30,000 was supposed to finish paying off the loans and cover his expenses while he and his buddies got the startup rolling. So without the $30,000, he couldn't move to San Francisco. He couldn't work for free at the start-up without having his loans paid off. He needed to go home and think things through. He took a right on Orion Street at the next stoplight. How could he get Chaos off his back? Where could he get $15,000? His car wasn't even worth that much. He shook his head. He was too smart for his own good. He'd thought that he'd get paid by Samantha — no harm in making a copy — that he'd pay his bills, move to California, start a new life. He hadn't thought about the downside.

He pulled into the parking lot of the Pine Gate apartments, a run-down, yellow brick, two-story apartment complex that was mainly populated by students from Orion College, and parked in front of his unit. He got out, keys in his hand. There was vomit in the snowbank beside the sidewalk. One of his neighbors must have been partying last night. As he approached his door, he saw motion in his peripheral vision. He turned. The two thugs that were with Jonny Chaos at the Silver Moose Tavern were on him.

Bobby, the guy with the shaved head who'd walked him to his car, grinned, his silver tooth black in his face, and slugged him in the stomach, knocking the wind out of him. Brandon folded up. The other guy, shorter and heavier, wearing a tiny red goatee, grabbed him by his hair and banged his head against the brick wall beside his door. His glasses came off one ear and fell down his face. Bobby kicked him behind the knee and he slid down the wall into the snow, blood running down the side of his face and from his nose.

Bobby shook his head. "You really aren't up for this, are you, Junior?" He glanced at his companion, who smiled like a cat sizing up a moth, and then crouched down and adjusted Brandon so that his back was against the wall. "The boss just wants you convinced of what you need to do. Are you convinced? Just nod your head."

Brandon nodded.

"That's great. Do what you need to do. Don't make us have to hunt you down. Standing in the cold makes us angry."

Bobby stood back up. A skinny, dark-haired woman with a gold ring in one nostril was standing in the door next door, watching. "What you looking at, sister? You want some of this?" Bobby grabbed his crotch. His companion laughed. The woman shut her door. Bobby turned back to Brandon. "You dropped your keys, bro. They're right there." He pointed to an indentation in the snow. "Don't sit there too long. That girl ain't going to feel sorry for you and come out here with chicken soup and loving." He tapped his companion on the shoulder. "Let's get out of here, Little Tom."

Brandon looked at the indentation where his keys were. If he sold his car, got $10,000 for it, then he'd only need $5,000. He put his glasses back on and crawled over to his keys. Where could he get $5,000?

Ronnie Franklin sat at his desk upstairs in his home office. He could hear Melanie bustling around down in the kitchen, working on Sunday supper, always a production for her. It was the one day of the week she cooked instead of just doctoring food out of cans or ordering take-out. A fat cookbook would be open on the kitchen island and the counters would be covered with dirty dishes and half-used containers of ingredients. And the result of all that effort would be something barely edible. It was a shame that she wasn't much of a cook. He shook his head. But it was really a shame she'd given up on sex. Sure, she'd cooperate. Lie there willingly. Orgasm, unless she was pretending. Who could tell? Well, back in the day she'd been hot for it. He smiled to himself. Pulling him into the bedroom, the hot tub, the garden shed. Begging for it. That was long ago. Back when Kat was a little girl. What would he miss about Melanie now? Her laugh when she watched a sit-com. Definitely. Her advice on office politics. Never failed. The way she could get Kat to quit pouting. Anything else?

He stroked his beard. He had to stop being morbid. Just because he told Angie that he was going to divorce Melanie didn't mean he had to. It was just talk; talk about the future. The kind of talk girlfriends loved. Right now he needed to focus on the present. Limit Melanie's spending and protect his assets. He turned back to his computer screen. He had just finished setting up his stock account to automatically start selling his Leapfrog shares beginning tomorrow. No one knew how Lilypad 5 would turn out. Even if it were a great product, it might not sell, and the company could still collapse. Taking a slight loss now was safer than risking his stock on Leapfrog's future. He had too many obligations. If the company went under, he needed as much cushion as possible. He reviewed the parameters. The settings were correct. He pressed the return key. After he had his money safely stashed away where Melanie couldn't get it, there would be plenty of time to decide what to do about his relationships.

"You've bought some new art." Brandon stood in Fred Olsen's living room, a glass of red wine in his hand.

Olsen shook his head. "No." He sipped his own wine. He was dressed, as usual, in black jeans and a black long-sleeve t-shirt. His red hair was mussed as if he'd recently taken off a stocking cap.

Brandon pointed to a large abstract print on the wall over the beat-up green sofa. "That's new."

"New two years ago."

"Has it been that long?"

Olsen smiled. "You haven't been here—well, you haven't been in my house since we graduated. That was three years ago. I bought this place two years ago. Treated myself to that print as a house-warming gift."

"How do you like living over your offices downtown?"

"It works for me. So, I haven't heard from you since you started at Leapfrog."

"Well, you know how the bosses are. They don't want us fraternizing with the competition."

"But now you call me out of the blue—I thought you'd forgotten all about me—say you have something to sell."

Brandon shrugged and nodded. "I need the cash."

Olsen pointed to the side of Brandon's face that had gotten scraped when Little Tom banged Brandon's head against the brick wall of his apartment building. "What happened there?"

"That's why I need the cash."

"You should have come in with me. You'd have your own cash right now."

Brandon glanced around the room at Olsen's rundown furnishings and wondered if Olsen had his student loans almost paid off. "Maybe you're right."

"I know I'm right." Olsen set his half-filled glass on the coffee table. "I'm all ears."

"I'm looking for five thousand."

"Must be some information to be worth that kind of money."

"To the right person, what I know is worth a lot more than that."

"Come on, I'm getting old waiting on you. Let's hear it."

"Maybe you've heard a rumor that Leapfrog is working on a data-mining program?"

Olsen nodded. "There's been some talk."

"Two points. One, the fire at Leapfrog on Friday was in the server room. The data-mining program was fried. It'll take them six months to resurrect it."

"Tough break."

"Two, the program was so buggy they were afraid it couldn't be fixed; that they would have to almost start over from scratch to get it to come out right."

"So the fire was a Godsend."

"There you have it, five thousand dollars' worth."

Olsen studied Brandon's face for a moment and then shook his head. "You are so full of shit."

"Full of shit? Everything I've told you is the truth."

"Your aunt put you up to this."

"Samantha? Why? Why would she want this info to get out?"

Olsen pointed his finger at Brandon. "I don't know. I do know that you'd get fired for telling me about Leapfrog's problems if your bosses didn't want you to."

"You owe me five thousand."

"Get out of here. I don't owe you anything. You should be ashamed. Coming around here, trading on our past friendship to try to screw me over—"

"How does the info I gave you hurt you, you cheap bastard?"

"Get out." Olsen pushed Brandon toward the door.

Wine sloshed out of Brandon's glass. He gulped the rest of his wine and slammed the glass down on the coffee table. "What does Samantha have to do with it?"

"Get out," Olsen said.

Brandon grabbed his coat off the coat rack by the door. "Asshole," he said over his shoulder. He clomped down the stairs. What was he going to do now? Think, think, think. He was grasping at straws. If Olsen had already opened Lilypad, he knew it was junk. Samantha's virus wouldn't slow him down for thirty minutes.

And if he hadn't opened it, why not? What was holding him back? Olsen just screwed over Samantha to get his hands on Lilypad. Why was he so suspicious? He should have had that program open, transferred, and the tablet thrown away before Samantha even got to the hospital. So, either he knew it was junk or he was too paranoid to open it. Either way he wasn't going to believe anything that Brandon said. The only way he would have paid was if he hadn't opened the program yet and he thought it was good. Which didn't make any sense. Brandon came out onto the sidewalk and slammed Olsen's downstairs door shut. God, where was he going to get the $5,000?

Olsen locked the upstairs door to his apartment. He went into the front door closet, dug around behind some old running shoes, and got out the tablet computer that he'd taken from Samantha. He set it on the coffee table, topped off his glass of wine, and looked at it. He hadn't yet examined the program; he hadn't even turned the tablet on. Why? Because the scenario was completely wrong. Samantha Bartel didn't do dishonest. And yet there she was at the food court with those two strangers. Who the hell were they? What would have happened if they had caught him on the stairs? Were they even supposed to catch him? Was it all an act to make him think he got away with it? He'd turn on the tablet, a tracking device would turn on, and the state police or the FBI or somebody would show up at his door, examine the tablet and find God-knows-what. And Brandon, he was lying about something, but what would that be? They'd had classes together, shared a few beers, but they'd never really been friends. Maybe he had a drug problem. Maybe his dealer beat him up.

Olsen went over to the desktop computer set up in the hutch on the other side of the living room, sat down, and set his wine glass on the shelf within reach. He put in his password, went online, and opened his tech blog. It was time "The Tech Master" told the world that Leapfrog's new data-mining program was junk. If it weren't, Leapfrog would roll it out and hold a demonstration to prove it was good. If it were, they'd put out a press release, stall, and try to buy some time until they could fix it. If they wouldn't hold a demonstration, he wasn't going to bother to turn on Samantha's tablet. And if they would, well, he'd have to think some more about it. Either way, he was getting that tablet out of his apartment.

6: Sorting the Players

On Monday, at midmorning, Leroy Smalls knocked on the open door to the office Stuart Jackson was using. Jackson, impeccably dressed in a tailored blue suit and silver tie, looked up from the laptop computer on his glass-topped desk. "There you are, Leroy. Thanks for stopping by. Have a seat."

Smalls sat down. Behind Jackson, a large double window looked out over the surrounding buildings. Except for the desk, two chairs, and a trashcan, the room was completely empty.

"How's your morning thus far?" Jackson asked.

"Still getting the fourth floor squared away, but we're almost there."

"Our stock price opened lower this morning. We haven't made any announcement regarding Lilypad's roll-out, so—"

"You're concerned about a possible leak."

"Exactly." Jackson nodded. "If we've got a leak, plug it. Fast. We have to maintain control of information if we're going to maintain control of our stock price."

"I'm on it. Anything else?"

"I'm counting on your discretion in investigating what happened with the surveillance cameras and the copy of Lilypad. We don't need any rumors of industrial espionage."

"I'm way ahead of you, Stuart."

"Thanks for taking care of the fire cleanup over the weekend."

Smalls got up. "You bet."

Smalls walked out of Jackson's office. He rubbed the back of his head. He'd have Stephanie make a show of examining phone logs and emails. That would put a damper on any leaking until he could figure out what was really going on. He walked by Ronnie Franklin's office and stopped. Ronnie had been acting suspiciously. And he had security clearance to all the equipment. It was a completely crazy idea, but maybe he should give Ronnie some rope and see what he did with it. He turned back to Franklin's office, knocked, and walked in. Franklin was working at his laptop. His black down coat was tossed over his file cabinet and the sleeves on his blue oxford shirt were rolled up. Papers and file folders were piled all over his desk. Smalls closed the door behind him and sat down. "Boss wants leaks plugged."

Franklin looked up. "So?"

Smalls sat back and crossed his legs. "You and Sam are up to something."

"What are you talking about?"

"Don't deny it. It's unprofessional. The two of you are doing something that's not fucking. And I bet with just a little bit of effort I could find out what this not fucking is."

"Why should I care?"

"Maybe you don't care. Maybe you don't care if Jackson finds out. Maybe we'll find out if you really don't care."

"Or?"

Smalls picked at his shoelace. "How slow do you want this investigation to go?"

Franklin closed his laptop and studied Smalls for a moment. "You must really be bored."

"Just trying to pay my bills."

"Me, too. I've got exactly the same problem. You can't get blood from a stone."

Smalls shrugged. "Well, if that's how you feel. I'll just go about my business; let the chips fall." He started to push himself up out of the chair.

Franklin held up his hand, motioning for Smalls to sit down. "How much bill paying are we talking about?"

Smalls smiled. "Two thousand dollars."

"Are you serious? That's what I've got to pay to keep you from picking at me while I'm trying to get Lilypad up and running?"

"Everyone's got their job to do."

"So while I'm saving your job, and everyone else's around here," Franklin circled his hand in the air, "I've got to pay you for the privilege?"

"No," Smalls said. "You've got to pay me for the privilege of not being investigated like everyone else. Assuming you aren't working against the company."

Franklin drummed his fingers on his desk. "Is this a one-time payment?"

Smalls nodded.

"Okay," Franklin said. "I'll have your money after lunch."

Small stood up. "Pleasure doing business with you."

Franklin opened his laptop and went back to work. Smalls closed the door on his way out. Two thousand dollars. Just like that. He was going to have to figure out what Ronnie and Sam were up to. Thus far, he'd assumed that the fire and security camera glitches were related. What if they weren't? What if they were separate problems that coincidentally happened at the same time? The camera problems could be connected to any number of minor scams. If Ronnie and Sam were selling out the company, he would have to turn them in. But if they weren't too far over the line, then maybe they'd be able to help him get back on his feet. A few thousand here and there would be a big help. He smiled to himself and straightened his necktie before he started down the steel staircase to the fourth floor.

Joe sat in his dark blue Ford Explorer across the street from the old First National Bank on the corner of Orion and Elm. "Paramount Design" was painted in large letters on the window. The lights were on, and he could see Fred Olsen moving around the office. He got out of the Ford, pulled the hood up on his green parka, waited for a break in traffic, and walked across the street at a diagonal, avoiding the furrows of dirty snow that had accumulated at the curbs. He tried the door to Paramount Design. It was unlocked, so he let himself in. The old bank counters and area dividers had been removed to open up the space, which currently contained several desktop computers and some folding tables stacked up with file folders and boxes of paper. Olsen looked up from a computer monitor near the back of the space, and said, "Sorry, I see people by appointment only. Go online to schedule an appointment."

"I guess you don't remember me," Joe said.

Olsen studied him quizzically.

Joe continued. "Guess you were too focused on Samantha, or maybe on dumping your decoy and getting the tablet."

Olsen just kept on looking at him.

Joe snapped his fingers. "Hello, wake up. At the food court in the mall on Saturday. Where Samantha broke her leg."

Olsen got up and took his phone out of his pants pocket. "You must have me confused with somebody else."

"Because Cloverdale is full of skinny, carrot-topped geeks."

Olsen started toward him. "I'm going to have to ask you to leave."

"You're going to have to pay us what you owe."

"I don't owe you anything. I'm calling the police." He started working the keypad on his phone.

In two steps, Joe snatched the phone from Olsen's hand and pitched it into the back of the room. Olsen grabbed the front of Joe's Parka. Joe grabbed the front of Olsen's shirt, jerked Olsen toward him, growled, and shoved his arms up between Olsen's, knocking Olsen's hands loose. Then he gave Olsen a hard push. Olsen took a step back, his mouth working as if he were trying to make sounds.

"You going to scream like a girl? You think the cops will protect you? You'll pay before we're through." Joe backed out the front door and walked off in the opposite direction from his SUV. The sun was melting the line of snow at the edge of the sidewalk and the building. He kept his head down, avoiding eye contact with passersby, and then ducked into an alley where he went through the back door of a Chinese restaurant. Three Asian men wearing cooks' whites were carrying trays of chopped vegetables from the stainless steel prep tables to the industrial gas range, setting up for lunch. Joe hustled by them and came out into the dining room.

The hostess, a young Asian woman wearing a black turtleneck sweater under a sleeveless maroon dress with dragons embroidered on it, followed him out from the kitchen. "We're not open yet."

He acted as if he didn't speak English and handed her five dollars. "Tea," he said. He sat down at a table where he could watch Paramount Design through the window. The hostess gave him a look like she thought he was crazy, but then sighed and brought him a pot of hot tea and a cup. He drank his tea, but Olsen didn't leave his office and the police didn't come.

What to do? He needed information. He left the restaurant through the kitchen and circled around the block to come up on Paramount Design from the side where the door to the upstairs apartment was. He knocked. No footsteps and no barking. He glanced up and down the street. No one was coming. He huddled in the doorway and picked the lock. At the top of the well-worn stairs, the door into the apartment hung open. He made a quick walk through the apartment, stepping very gently so as not to make noise that would raise Olsen's suspicion downstairs. The living room was old furniture and a wannabe abstract print on the wall. The contents of the bedroom—the linens, the bed frame, the dresser, and the clothes in the closet— weren't good enough to sell at the Salvation Army. The kitchen was the usual load of thrown-together, mismatched crap. There was nothing of value lying around: no cash, no jewelry, no real art. Computers just weren't worth the trouble of stealing anymore.

He and Tess could annoy Olsen by stealing his car or setting fire to this dump, but that would just increase their risk without increasing their opportunity to make money. Joe went into the bathroom and urinated, but he didn't flush the toilet or wash his hands. He just wiped them on the still-damp bath towel, almost as an afterthought. On his way back down, he walked the edges of the dusty stairs to keep the steps from creaking. He pulled up the hood of his parka before he opened the front door and peeked outside. All clear. He crossed the street to his Explorer. This escapade had been a complete waste of time.

Melanie Franklin sat in the outer office of Glenmore and Stowe, P.C., Attorneys at Law. She hadn't taken off her tan wool coat. A large print of a spring landscape—newly budded leaves, bright flowers, and playful birds—hung on the far wall. Light classical music wafted in through the ceiling speakers. The receptionist, a thin, young African-American woman in a black skirt suit and white shirt, a diamond solitaire engagement ring prominently displayed on her hand, brought Melanie a cup of coffee in a ceramic mug that advertised the bank across the street. Melanie looked at her own rings—the gold band and the tenth anniversary diamond ring—sighed, took the cup in both hands and blew on the coffee. An athletic-looking middle-aged man with a cleft chin and steel gray hair, dressed in a charcoal pinstripe suit, came through from the inner offices. "Ms. Franklin? I'm Jeff Gardener. Come on back."

He held the door for her. "First door on the left."

She went into his office, walnut built-in bookcase with matching desk, set her coffee down on the glass protecting his desk top, and slipped out of her coat before she sat down. Gardener closed the door and sat down in the high-back black leather chair behind his desk. A yellow legal pad and a pen lay on the desk in front of him. "How can I help you?"

Melanie picked up her coffee and took a sip. "Thank you for seeing me so quickly. This is hard to talk about."

"Take your time."

She set the coffee cup down and looked at the wire dog sculpture on the corner of Gardener's desk. "I think my husband is having an affair."

Gardener frowned and nodded.

"It's just a suspicion. But now he's talking about changing jobs."

"I see."

"Maybe I'm just being paranoid, but I'm afraid he might be getting ready to leave me."

"And he's the sole breadwinner?"

"Yes."

"Ms. Franklin, we're in a no-fault state. You don't need a reason to start divorce proceedings and you don't have to move out of your home."

"I don't know if I want a divorce. Our daughter has another year of high school."

He nodded. "I understand."

"What should I do to protect myself?"

"Financially?"

"Yes."

"Have you been monitoring your jointly-held bank accounts, mutual funds, stocks, bonds? Sometimes a person who's planning to leave will start hiding money."

"Hiding money?"

Gardener sat back in his chair. "Uh-huh, hiding money to keep it out of the divorce, or to cover up expenses that are part of a secret relationship. The bills are all paid, as usual, but money for discretionary items just seems a little tighter, and there doesn't seem to be any reason why. Do you follow me?"

"I think so."

"Of course, if this is what's going on, everything he manages to hide will be hard to track down. But if you want to try to wait until your daughter finishes school, keep an eye on the assets, and if you become concerned that something fishy is going on, move the cash to a new bank and call me."

"Okay."

"Bottom line, it's your decision. You tell us what you want us to do, and we'll do everything possible to make sure you get a good outcome."

"Thank you, Mr. Gardener."

"But you've got to be very careful. Once the horse is out of the barn . . ."

"I understand."

They shook hands. Melanie put her coat back on. Gardener walked her back down the hall to the outer office. Out on the sidewalk, she thought she might cry, but she just sniffled and wiped her nose. The sun felt warm on her face. She took a deep breath. She should probably run an errand or two while she was downtown. She found two quarters in her clutch purse, fed the parking meter, and started down the street to the coffee shop where she liked to buy the ground coffee they used at home. Was Ronnie cheating on her? She must believe it; she'd just said it out loud. Would she really leave him if he were? She really wasn't sure. Would she stay if he admitted the truth? She stopped at the intersection to wait for the walk light. Would she ever be able to trust him again? Did she trust him now? Maybe money really was tighter than she thought; his end-of-year bonus had been a lot smaller than usual, but they had that new

CEO, Stuart what's-his-name. A group of men and women gathered around her at the curb. Cars stopped at the crosswalk. The walk light came on. She scurried across with the crowd. The PourAway Coffee Shop was on the corner. She pushed through the door. It was 11:40 a.m. The tables were full and a long line snaked back toward the door. She got in line. The money was what was making her suspicious. She had to follow the money; then she would know if something were really wrong. And then, maybe, she would be able to decide what she should do.

At 12:15 p.m. Tess was in Samantha's office at Leapfrog Technologies, sitting behind her standard gray metal desk and going through the drawers. Samantha had called in sick, so Carol had asked Tess to help answer the phones and run the copier in the reception area that morning, since she wasn't cleared to work at a computer. But now it was the lunch hour and the offices were more or less empty. On Samantha's desk, to the left, was a framed photo of her deceased parents, shriveled, ancient versions of Samantha, looking happy and frail on a windy beach somewhere. To the right was a carved, wooden head with a pair of computer glasses sitting on its nose. As Tess sifted through the desk drawers, all she found were office supplies and files of project notes. Samantha's life was almost too clean. There was nothing in this office or in her desk that shouldn't have been there, which made it hard to believe that she was actually involved in any criminal activity. There might be something on the laptop sitting on the center of the desk, but Tess wasn't going to waste her time testing passwords. Samantha's password would definitely be random letters and numbers.

Tess took one final look around the office before she shut the door. Twelve thirty. Plenty of time. She went to the stairwell and listened downstairs. Still quiet. She picked the lock on Franklin's office door. Framed awards hung on one wall, thick dust on the tops of the frames. Piles of file folders and loose papers covered the desktop. She sat down behind the desk to orient herself, and then riffled through the stacks, looking for anything out of the ordinary. Nothing. She started through the drawers. File drawer: more of the same. Top drawer: usual office supplies and bits of junk. Second drawer: hello. Pint of vodka lying on its side, half-full, and a smartphone, not company issue. She opened the phone and went to the address book. Not much there: the wife, the kid, pizza, Samantha, Angie. Which made this Angie a VIP. Tess copied down the phone number and put the phone away. The elevator dinged. She rushed out of the office and shut the door. As the elevator opened, Franklin looked up from unzipping his black down jacket. He smiled through his beard. "Looking for me?"

Tess smiled back. "Actually, I was." She dropped a pen, turned her back to him as she bent down to pick it up, and unbuttoned the top two buttons of her pink blouse to expose a peek of her matching lacy bra. Then she stood up and waited for him to walk over. When he stopped, she took a step toward him, getting in close. He didn't back away. She could smell alcohol on his breath. She looked up into his face to give him a good look at her cleavage. "I was hoping to talk with you about any possible job opening here."

"Really?"

"I graduate in the spring."

"Congratulations." He put his hand on her shoulder. "Why don't we go into my office?"

He unlocked the door and ushered her in. "I'm kind of surprised you aren't discussing this with Samantha."

She sat on the edge of his desk and let her skirt ride up a little. "I like Samantha. I'm glad to have the opportunity to learn from her, but I tend to get along better with men than with women, know what I mean?"

He looked her up and down and nodded. "Absolutely." He shut his office door. When he turned around, she was standing in front of him. She grabbed his red necktie, pulled his face down to hers, and kissed him. "Whoa," he said.

"Oh," she said, taking a step back, "I'm sorry. If there's a misunderstanding —"

"No, no," he said, "everything's okay. I was just a little surprised. Would you like a drink?" He threw his down jacket over the extra chair in the back corner of his office, and took the pint of vodka out of his desk drawer. "I'm sorry; I don't have any glasses in here."

"That's okay," she said, "I'm an ex-sorority girl." She drank from the bottle, choked and spluttered. He laughed. She handed him the bottle. He drank, capped the bottle, and set it on the desk. Then he took her by the arm and pulled her to him. "If there's a problem, now's the time to say so."

"There's no problem."

"We're going to have to be quiet."

She laughed softly. He pushed her up against the wall. She kissed him hungrily while she unbuckled his belt. He pulled up her skirt and grabbed at her pink thong. She jerked his jeans down. She gripped his shoulders and lifted herself up onto his hips. "Think you can hold me?" she whispered.

"Uh-huh."

"We'll see," she said.

Ten minutes later, Tess stood facing the office door. She wiggled her thong up and smoothed her skirt down. Franklin was sitting on the edge of his desk, breathing hard, with his jeans around his ankles. She turned to look at him, smiled playfully, grabbed the front of her bra cups and gave them a tug. "Time to pull your pants up, lover boy. I've got to go."

He pulled his jeans and underwear up all together and was buckling his belt when she crossed to him and pecked him on the cheek. "I hope this interview was as good for me as it was for you," she said.

"You definitely made an impression," he said.

She smiled brightly, fluffed her hair, and turned on her heels. She left the door open on her way out.

Franklin looked around his office to see if anything were obviously out of place, and then straightened the photograph of Melanie, Kat, and himself taken for the church directory two years ago. Melanie and he looked the same, but Kat was a girl, instead of being the young woman she was now. He sat behind his desk, neatened a pile of file folders, and turned on his computer. He felt suddenly at odds with himself. Sex with Sam's intern? God, was this what a midlife crisis was like? This wasn't like him at all. If word got out, Stuart would fire him faster than he could say "sexual harassment." It never would have happened if Sam hadn't called in sick. What had he been thinking? He brought his hand to his face; Tess's scent was on his fingers. He shook his head. That was the problem. He hadn't been thinking. But Tess wasn't going to tell anyone. She was trading favors. He put his hands on his desk and took a deep breath. What was done was done. He just needed to make sure it never happened again. He entered his computer password and opened his email account.

He'd finished with his emails and was deep in an examination of a proposal for a new product that one of the young programmers hoped to use to boost her career when Smalls rapped on his open door with the back of his hand. "Just came in the building. Thought you might like a cup of real coffee." He was holding two throwaway cups with the Wholly Roasters logos on their sides.

"Hey, hey," Franklin said. "Come on in."

Smalls handed him one of the cups and sat down. Smalls popped the cover off his coffee, blew across the top of the cup, and took a sip. "You got something for me?"

Franklin nodded. He had a nagging doubt about giving Leroy the money. Leroy had never asked him for a payment before. What was different now? What would he do if Leroy asked for more? Leroy was good at his job. Once he started probing, he'd certainly find Angie and the $50,000 Franklin had taken to pay the thieves. But his affair had nothing to do with the company and the money could easily be explained away. Really, this problem was all Stuart's fault. He was pushing Leroy's buttons, making him dig. But as soon as Lilypad was fixed, Stuart would start focusing on other things and Leroy would get busy investigating something else. Leroy was a manageable problem. It was all about making Lilypad a success. At least Leroy hadn't shown up while Tess was there. That would have been a catastrophe. Franklin rolled his chair back to reach into the outer pocket of his down jacket and took out a bank envelope. He handed it across to Smalls.

Smalls set his coffee on Franklin's desk and thumbed through the crisp one hundred dollar bills. "Thanks."

Franklin studied Smalls's face. "So we're good? This is the end of it?"

"We're set." Smalls stood up and slipped the envelope into the inside chest pocket of his blue blazer. "Have a good afternoon."

It was 5:45 p.m. Ronnie Franklin closed his laptop and looked over the piles of paperwork on his desk. Smalls had gotten the cleanup finished on the fourth floor. The Lilypad team had done forensics on the burned server and scoured their computers for undeleted parts of the data-mining program. Little did they know that he had a complete copy on his laptop. Julie at Arrow Computer had guaranteed that the new equipment would arrive first thing tomorrow. Janie in tech maintenance knew her job depended on having the new server online before lunch. And Sam would be back on the job—maybe not full strength, but at least hobbling around. So he was going to have to spend the evening deciding how to change the membership of the Lilypad team to get some fresh thinking and innovative coding. He sorted through the file folders on his desk, pulled his messenger bag up into his lap, and slid three folders and his laptop into the bag. He was going to have to stop drinking at lunch. Made him slow in the afternoon.

Besides, he never would have screwed Tess if he hadn't been half in the bag. Get her a job here? When she pulled up her skirt, her chances went from maybe to no way. He couldn't have her around here wanting to take things further or holding it over his head whenever she wanted a favor. He turned off his lights and locked his door. As he was walking toward the elevator, Stuart Jackson called out to him. When was he going to quit micromanaging and go back to the main office? He looked in Jackson's door. Jackson was sitting at his desk in his shirtsleeves; several file folders of papers open before him.

"Glad I caught you. Shut the door."

Franklin shut the door and sat down. "What's up?"

Jackson looked at him over the top of his steel-framed glasses. "Our stock has been slipping all day. This morning I tasked Leroy with plugging leaks. About an hour ago, Carol showed me a blog that says the fire was a ruse, that Lilypad is junk and that's why the rollout has been postponed."

"Whose blog?"

"The Tech Master."

Franklin shook his head. "The Tech Master? Are you serious? That guy is the stupidest crank—"

"He's getting plenty of hits."

"Stuart, you saw all the progress reports. You saw the damage. Pull in programmers and question them if you like, but all that's going to do is feed the leak."

"I had to ask."

Franklin nodded. "You are right, though. We've got to deal with these accusations head on. So we need to post footage of the fire damage, thank the company that did the cleanup. We can't convince conspiracy nuts, but we can convince reasonable people."

"That sounds like a start."

"If that doesn't quash the rumors, we'll figure out our next step."

"How much progress have you made today?"

"We'll be up and running on the new server by tomorrow afternoon. The programmers are already assembling the bits and pieces off their machines."

"We need your people on this around the clock. You see how the publicity is going. We've got to stabilize the stock price. And we've got to have Lilypad up as soon as possible if we're going to turn this company around."

Franklin pointed to his messenger bag. "I'm on it. Just eating supper with my family before I get back to work. Anything else?"

"Samantha was out today."

"Broke her leg on Saturday. I've been keeping her up to date."

"I didn't realize. Should I give her a call?"

"She'll be in tomorrow."

"Great. Have a good evening, Ronnie. I know there's a lot riding on your shoulders now, but when we get through this, the bonuses will show the effort."

"Thanks, Stuart."

Franklin continued down the hall to the elevator. If only he could get the right programmers together, get the right synergy, he could save Lilypad, be the hero, ride that success to a much better job somewhere else. But the timeline was short. If Lilypad were hopeless, he had to be at the new job before anyone discovered that Leapfrog was history. So he really was going to have to work twenty-four seven on pushing Lilypad out and on finding a job without being caught at it. Because as soon as Stuart heard he was on the market, he'd be fired and escorted out of the building, just as surely as if Stuart found out he sabotaged Lilypad. The elevator opened. Of course, selling off his Leapfrog stock was his ace in the hole. It gave him more room to maneuver. If they couldn't fix Lilypad and he couldn't find a new job, at least he'd still have his retirement money. But that was just a contingency. Lilypad was fixable. He patted his bag. The answers were all in here. He just had to sort them out.

Joe and Tess sat in a back booth in a downtown sports bar. Happy hour was in full swing. A crowd of twenty-somethings in business wear hugged the bar. Classic rock favorites blared from the speakers. Everyone was yelling to be heard over the music. Joe and Tess sat on the same side of the booth with their backs to the back wall, Joe with one arm around her shoulders and the other hand holding an Old Fashioned. She leaned against him, her near hand on his thigh, her other hand holding a bottle of Bud light. She was speaking into his ear. "Almost got caught in Franklin's office. But I found an extra phone, not Leapfrog, and copied a suspicious number."

"He suspect anything?"

"I told him I was looking for him to ask about a job. Fucked him to close the deal."

"You're on the top of your game. I came up empty-handed with Olsen. Denied taking the tablet and there was nothing of value in his apartment. We could threaten his life, but I don't think it would make any difference. What about Samantha?"

"Clean as a whistle. Makes her whole play seem loco, know what I mean?"

"Come on, honey. A player has tells."

She shook her head. "Franklin is a train wreck waiting to happen. That horndog is up to something, even if he's not in this game. But Samantha? The angles are all wrong."

"So there's nothing?"

"There's a rumor at work that she's in the closet, but that's so much air. Just people judging the middle-aged single woman."

Joe sipped his drink. "She doesn't sound seducible. This gig is tapping out sooner than I thought."

"Check into the phone number?"

"Might as well."

Joe's phone rang. He took his arm from around Tess and looked at the phone's face. Brandon. He answered it. "Talk to me."

"Hey, Joe, I need your help."

Joe smiled. "Is that a fact?"

"You know Jonny Chaos?"

"Yeah."

"He's after me."

"Then you better pay him."

"I don't have the money."

"Then you better leave town."

"The theft was all crap. You know that, right?"

Joe motioned to Tess. She put her ear up to the other side of the phone. "What's that?" Joe asked. "It's kind of noisy in here."

"The theft of Lilypad 5. It was all bullshit. It doesn't work. Stealing it was just to buy time so Samantha and her boss wouldn't get fired."

"Says who?"

"That's why Chaos is after me. I made a copy and sold it to him."

"And now you don't have the juice to pay him back."

"Will you help me?"

"If you're telling the truth, I'll see what I can do. Stay out of sight for a few days."

"I'll get a motel room."

"Whatever." Joe hung up. He set his phone on the table in front of him. "Motherfucker. Did you hear all that?"

"Think he's telling the truth?"

"If so, it means Samantha's plan was to cheat Olsen to pay us. I don't like being played."

"You're not planning on helping the kid?" Tess asked.

He smiled thoughtfully. "So long as he thinks we might help him, he'll do some favors for us. And Jonny's a loose cannon.

We might be able to take advantage of that." He sipped his Old Fashioned. "But first we need to lean on Samantha. If this job was always a load of crap, there might be some money she's squirreled back." He put his phone in his pocket and gulped down the last of his drink. "You ready?"

She nodded. They slid out of the booth and put their coats on. Before they'd walked halfway to the door, a foursome that had been crowded at the bar was already sitting down in the booth and motioning toward the server.

Melanie Franklin, dressed in her plum-colored track suit, sat in front of her desktop computer at the brown granite-topped built-in desk in the kitchen after supper, the dishwasher whooshing behind her, studying the family stock account, trying to figure out what was going on with the Leapfrog Technologies stock. It was like trying to read a serious science textbook when she hadn't read a science textbook in a long, long time. She was trying to remember what the technical language meant while stringing together what the sentences meant. Finally, she reached up into the cookbook shelf, got a note pad, and started writing out the meanings of the technical terms so that she could refer to the meanings when she got confused. Kat, dressed in her gold and blue dance team cover-ups, came up behind her. "Hey, Mom."

She turned. "Hi, honey."

"What you doing?"

"Trying to figure out this stock account."

"Where's Dad?"

"Up in his office."

Kat looked over her mother's shoulder. "That number's been going down all day." She pointed at the Leapfrog Technologies screen. "You should talk to Dad." She kissed her mom on the cheek. "I've got practice. I won't be too late."

"Thanks, honey. Drive safely."

Melanie studied the screen. Kat was right. The Leapfrog Technologies stock had lost a little value, but the number of shares was also down. She got out her cell phone and called Ronnie upstairs. "Hey, honey, have you got a minute."

"Sure. I need a break from this program anyway."

"What's up with the stock account? It looks like we've been losing Leapfrog shares."

"The stock lost a little value today, so I'm guessing a preset program sold some shares to take the losses. The money will be automatically reinvested. It's a tax thing. And we're still trying to get some car money. Want me to come down and look?"

"No, don't bother. I was just curious."

"Okay, anything else?"

"No. Hope you don't have to work too late."

"Fallout from the fire. A couple of days should set things right."

Melanie ended the call and set her phone next to her mouse. So now she had to write down what the shares were worth and multiply that by the number sold and then see if that amount resurfaced in cash or new shares of something else, either in the stock account or mutual fund account. Even then she wouldn't have the exact amount unless she tracked the change in price all day against the numbers sold. Her head started pounding at a spot behind her left eye. She put her hand over the eye. God, this was so hard. She just couldn't make her brain work anymore. She logged out of the account. She'd finish this in the morning when she was fresh. Right now she needed to take some ibuprofen and get ready for bed.

Samantha hobbled across her living room, her baby blue robe open over her pink-striped nightgown, and leaned on her crutches to open her front door. Joe and Tess stood on her concrete stoop. Her mouth dropped open. She looked from one to the other. A cold blast of wind rustled her nightgown and brought up goose bumps on her ankles.

"Surprised to see us?" Joe said.

"Aren't you going to invite us in?" Tess said.

Samantha shuffled back.

"No worries," Tess said. "You sit down. We'll close the door and hang up our coats."

Joe bolted the front door. They tossed their coats onto the blue corduroy chair next to the matching sofa. "Sit, sit," Tess said.

Samantha sat back down in her place on the sofa and propped her casted leg up on the leather cube. A basketball game was on the TV. "Can I get you something to drink?"

Joe nodded. "We'll help ourselves." Tess sat down next to Samantha. Joe called from the kitchen. "Tess, beer or diet coke?"

"Beer," she hollered back. She turned to Samantha. "Anything for you?"

"I'm fine."

"Sam's fine," she yelled. She picked up the remote and turned off the TV.

Joe came back into the living room with two bottles of beer. He handed one to Tess and then sat on the arm of the chair where their coats lay. He looked at Tess expectantly.

Tess drank from her beer and then patted Samantha's hand. "We recently heard some things that concern us. You know, about our little project. Do you have anything you want to tell us? I just want to warn you that Joe can be pretty hard when he loses his temper."

"What did you hear?"

"No, no, no, that's exactly the kind of thing that makes Joe angry. See, it makes him think you're doing damage control instead of telling the truth. What he, and I, want is for you to tell us the truth about what we got involved in, so we don't end up blindsided and in jail."

Samantha looked up at Joe. He looked down at his knees and rolled the cold beer bottle back and forth across his forehead. Tess shifted her gaze. "Getting a headache, baby?"

Joe looked up. His mustache made his frown look evil. "I hope not."

Samantha held her hands up. "I always meant for you to get your money."

"No doubt," Joe said.

"The plan was to make the trade with Olsen, give you your cash, everyone forgets they ever met."

Tess patted Samantha's hand. "But?"

Samantha looked at Tess. "You saw how it went."

"And you've got no money to pay us?"

Samantha shook her head.

"Then you've got to tell us the truth; give us the chance to earn," Joe said.

Samantha looked up at him. "So that's what this is all about?"

"That's what it's always about. Making money. We're not doing this to fill the day or because our feelings got hurt. All you've got to trade is the plan, so now you've got to tell us everything from the beginning so we can figure out how to get our fifty thousand."

Samantha pulled a tissue from the box on the arm of the sofa and blew her nose. "Lilypad wasn't ready for the rollout. It was too buggy. Something in one of the underlying programs wasn't right, but we couldn't fix it in time."

Tess smiled. "See, that's not so hard."

"Why not postpone?" Joe asked.

"This product is make or break for the company. The last two products didn't sell as well as expected. If the board of directors found out Lilypad wasn't ready, I'd be fired for sure. All I have left is my company stock and my job. I've spent everything else. I paid for my parents' nursing home care. You don't have any idea. It was more expensive than college. I went into aggressive positions in the stock market to make up the difference; then the market crashed. I lost most of that. I'm at the end of my rope. If I get fired at my age, I won't be able to get another job like this one. My retirement is gone. Why else would I get involved in this mess?"

Joe started walking back and forth in front of Tess and Samantha, the beer bottle in his hand. "You aren't in this by yourself. Who else is in it?"

"Just Ronnie Franklin."

"Nobody else?"

"No one. The CEO would have fired us to save his job. The kids could all get new jobs, maybe even promotions. Brandon was just in it for the cash. He thought that Lilypad was good."

"Does Franklin know who we are?"

"No. And he doesn't want to know."

Tess smirked. "Because right now all roads point to you."

"That's right," Samantha said.

Joe pointed at Samantha with his beer bottle. "How did you and Franklin keep the others from finding out?"

She shrugged. "The work was compartmentalized. People see what they want to see. The boss says 'good job' and everybody pats themselves on the back. Maybe that's the one place I caught a break." She looked from Joe to Tess. "What are you going to do?"

"Relax," Joe said. "You fired or in jail doesn't help us. As long as you cooperate, you'll be fine." He drank from his beer and then set it on an end table. "Tess, let's get out of here."

Tess got up and grabbed her coat. "See you at work tomorrow."

The stars were out, shining brightly in the icy cold. Joe and Tess could see their breath. They zipped up their coats and pulled on their gloves as they walked down Samantha's front steps. "Careful," Joe said, "there's a patch of ice." Tess mumbled something and stepped around it. They were quiet until they got into their Explorer and started the engine.

"So," Tess said, "what are we going to do?"

"Stories are consistent."

"Yeah."

"Samantha is probably good at what she does, but I don't think she really knows what's going on and I don't think we'll get any more money from her," Joe said.

"Yeah, according to her, the bosses are running on fear and adrenaline—so it's Franklin? You think he's devious enough to get away with fucking me and pretending he didn't know who I really was?"

"He's our most likely target. Let's back-trace that phone number you screwed him for. Find out who Angie is and where she lives."

Joe pulled out into traffic. Tess got out her laptop, went online, found an address. "She's at 1806B Ridgeview Avenue."

"Ridgeview? Out to the south?"

"Let me Google it." She checked Google maps. "Yeah, it's across from the golf course."

"Well, let's check it out."

There were few cars on the streets and the stoplights were cooperative. It seemed everyone was at home after a hard

Monday at work. On Ridgeview Avenue, the chain-link fence of Cloverdale Golf and Country Club was on their right and an assortment of coffee shops, chain restaurants, and apartment complexes were on the left. "Next left," Tess said.

Joe turned into the red-tile-roofed Ridgeview Apartments. They followed the numbers around until they came to 1806B, which was located within easy walking distance of the clubhouse and outdoor pool. They parked in a visitor's spot. Joe glanced at Tess. "Ready to take a look?"

"The light is on."

"Doesn't mean anyone is home. Just a peek. Might see something interesting."

They got out of the Explorer and pulled up their hoods. Streetlamps lit the parking lot, and a few of the apartments had their outside lights on. The sidewalks were all scraped clean, the snow piled in the right of way with snow-thrower efficiency. "Hate to walk in the snow; leave tracks," Joe said.

Tess glanced down at her high heels. "I'm not wearing shoes for it anyway."

"If she comes to the door — Church of Jesus Love?"

"Just wanting a few minutes to spread the word."

They walked up the sidewalk to Angie's front door. Tess stood and glanced around like she was waiting for Angie to come to the door. Joe stepped onto the gravel between the wall and the bushes, crouched down, and peeked through the window. Angie, dressed in blue yoga pants and a green and blue sweater, sat on the sofa watching TV. Joe stepped back to the sidewalk, tapped Tess on the shoulder, and pointed toward their SUV. They walked back down the sidewalk to the parking lot. "Well?" Tess said.

"Doesn't look like his sister, so I make her for the honey pot. We need to have a look in there when she's at work."

They got back into the Explorer. "What do you think's in there?" Tess asked.

"Don't know." Joe started the SUV. "This is the deal. Olsen is a dead end. He's got nothing except his image. Samantha's a wash, but we can use her. Franklin seems to be calling the shots, so we've got to find a way to put pressure on him to see what we can squeeze out. There's still money on the table. I can feel it. And you know me; I hate to leave money on the table."

Leroy Smalls sat on a stool at the bar in the Ace-King-Queen Sports Bar. The Celtics-Bulls game had just finished. He'd lost on the point spread. James, dreadlocks hanging in his face and the sleeves of his white shirt rolled up to his elbows, was washing the glasses from the two tables that had cleared out immediately after the game. No one else was in the bar. Charlene, the waitress, a twenty-one-year-old redhead wearing a white apron over a short black skirt and a white mini t-shirt, leaned up in the servers' station with a bored, dejected look on her face. "Cheer up, baby," James said. "At least you'll go home early."

She gave him a look like he still lived with his mother. "I don't need home early. I need tip money to pay bills and buy groceries."

"Never happen on a Monday, except during playoffs. So don't let the other girls crowd you out in May."

Smalls shook the ice in his glass. "Give me one more; then I got to go."

"Sure, Pops." James poured a generous rum and coke, slid it across the bar to Smalls, and pulled six dollars off the stack of bills sitting on the bar in front of Smalls.

The door opened, Charlene looked up, hopeful, and then sighed. A short white man with large glasses and a thin comb-over walked up to the bar. "Leroy."

Smalls looked over his shoulder. "Gary. I thought you'd be here earlier to watch the game with me."

Gary kept his green parka on, but sat on the stool next to Smalls. James looked at him expectantly.

"What'll you have?" Smalls asked.

"Shot of Jack."

Smalls nodded at James. James set a shot glass down in front of Gary and poured Jack Daniel's whiskey up to the rim. Gary nodded his appreciation. Smalls pushed a ten- dollar bill toward James, who took it and brought back four dollars in change.

Gary carefully lifted his shot glass and took a sip. "Ready to settle up?"

Smalls reached into the inside chest pocket of his blue blazer, took out the bank envelope he'd gotten from Franklin, and set it on the table in front of Gary. Then he reached into his front pants pocket, pulled out a roll of money, and counted out $1,500. "What I owed, plus the weekend and today. I make that at thirty-five hundred."

Gary looked around the bar.

"Completely safe here," Smalls said. "Besides, I always go armed."

Gary looked in the envelope at the $2,000, took the $1,500 from Smalls, added them together, and put the bulging envelope into his front pants pocket. "That makes us square. I appreciate your business." He drank off the shot of whiskey and stood up. "Thanks again, Leroy."

Gary left the bar. Smalls looked at his rum and coke, the light refracting through the ice cubes to create highlights in the brown liquid, took a drink and looked back up at the TV. A razor blade commercial was playing. A man in a white t-shirt was shaving his perfect face while the voice-over discussed the lubrication of the multi-blade razor system. Smalls took another drink. The $2,000 he'd gotten from Ronnie had been a big help, but the $1,500 from his own bank account had cleaned him out. He had, what? Maybe $200 in his pocket? He still needed to pay the $1,200 he'd lost with his other bookie over the weekend. His credit cards were maxed out. He needed a win. A big win. He had to catch up his mortgage next month. He finished his drink, left three dollars on the bar, and got up.

"See you later, Pops," James said.

Smalls waved in reply. Maybe he could borrow some more money against his life insurance.

7: Shaking the Tree

On Tuesday at 10:00 a.m., Franklin sat in his office with his door open, concentrating on the notes he'd gotten from the new Lilypad team, which was busy examining the program line by line to fix the bugs and to figure out which sections needed to be altered to make the program more effective. As they finished each section, he compared it to the original to make sure they weren't just traveling down the same well-worn path. Fresh faces and fresh eyes. The promise of fixing the program, keeping his job, and getting out from under the problem of job-hunting. He could hear Samantha out in the hall clomping around on her crutches. He wondered what her reaction would be when she saw these notes. He heard Tess's voice. He planned on avoiding her today, if he could do it without seeming like he was doing it.

His personal telephone vibrated from his desk drawer. He looked at the face. Unknown number. Probably Angie calling from a work phone. "Hello?"

"Ronnie Franklin?" A man's voice said.

"Who is this?"

"We know what you've done."

"Really? What's that?"

"You destroyed the server."

"Who are you?"

"You owe me fifty thousand. You want Stuart Jackson to find out you sabotaged Lilypad 5?"

"I don't know what you're talking about. We had a fire. Lucky the whole building didn't burn down. If you know

85

anything about criminal activity, you should notify Mr. Jackson and the police."

"You benefited."

"You're crazy." Franklin hung up. Samantha called him when? Saturday. He counted on his fingers. It took the thieves three days to connect the dots to him and to get his private phone number. But how? How did they get the phone number? He called Samantha.

"Sam. I just got a call from a friend of yours."

"A friend?"

"The potato man."

"Really?"

"Did you tell them about me?"

"No. They only got the info they needed to do the job."

"Have you been in contact with them?"

"Not since Saturday."

"Damn. Well, it doesn't change anything. Have you read the notes from the new team?"

"Not yet."

"Things are looking up. We need to stall the potato man. Maybe he'll decide to buy his potatoes somewhere else."

"Maybe we should give him the potatoes."

"Only as a last resort. Call me if he contacts you. Read the team notes. We'll talk later."

"Do you actually believe he's going away?"

"We'll talk later."

Franklin sat back in his chair and looked out his door into the hall. Realistically, he had a two-week window. If Lilypad was still on the right track in two weeks, he wasn't looking for a new job and it made sense to pay off the thieves. If not, he had to find a new job and Sam was on her own. He turned back to his computer, scrolled down to where he had left off and continued reading the team's notes.

At 12:30 he got up, stretched his arms overhead to flex his back, pulled on his parka and left his office, locking the door behind him. He walked down the steel staircase to the third floor and out through the reception area. "Carol, I'm going to the gym. Be back before two."

Carol, computer glasses perched on her nose, glanced up from her computer screen and nodded. "Enjoy."

He walked out the glass doors to the parking deck and got in his Volvo. His red nylon gym bag was in the backseat. When he pulled out of the parking deck and turned onto the street, Joe, waiting in his Ford Explorer in the metered, on-street parking, followed him. The sky was overcast; the traffic was stop-and-go until they passed the intersection with Orion Avenue. They continued south and were soon on Ridgeview Avenue — Cloverdale Golf and Country Club on the right, the red-tile-roofed Ridgeview apartments on the left. Franklin turned into the Ridgeview Apartments, parked in front of the clubhouse, and walked over to Angie's apartment building. Joe pulled into a numbered spot for a resident in the middle of the lot, sat for five minutes watching the door to Angie's apartment, and then drove away.

Joe and Tess stood in the entry to the Silver Moose Tavern. It was still happy hour. Men and women in dirty work clothes crowded the bar and the tables, and the Country and Rock top-forty jukebox couldn't compete with the din of conversation. Tess was wearing dark blue leggings and a white scoop-necked blouse with a long pink cardigan sweater under her gray overcoat. Joe was wearing his blue suit with a white shirt. His parka was unzipped. They stuck out like missionaries at a Hell's Angels convention. "So this is where Chaos hangs out?" Tess asked.

"That's what they say," Joe replied.

Joe took Tess's hand and led the way to Jonny Chaos's booth at the back. When he saw Chaos's two bodyguards, tattooed thugs wearing brown work coats, standing at the bar nursing beers, he got his free hand around the butt of the pistol in his parka pocket. The taller one, who had a shaved head and the neck tattoo, stepped between Joe and Chaos's booth, his eyes dead, his hands balled up into fists, while his partner, stockier and sporting a tiny red goatee, shifted his right hand into the pocket of his coat. Joe looked up into the taller one's face, still holding Tess's hand and still holding the pistol in his pocket. "Just here to talk."

The thug's mouth barely moved. "If he wants to talk." He looked over his shoulder. Chaos shrugged inside his black wool overcoat.

Joe let Tess into the booth first, and then slid in beside her. Jonny Chaos pushed his greasy hair out of his eyes. The overhead spotlight lit up the rings on his fingers. "Grifters."

Joe nodded.

"Why are we talking?"

"You're dogging Brandon Bartel."

"So? This is my town. I'll dog who I want."

"You can kill the kid for all I care, but it won't get you your money; he's just the middleman. A guy named Ronnie Franklin, one of the bosses at Leapfrog Technologies, is behind the whole thing."

"What do you care if I get paid?"

"I don't care. We're just trying to make a living here. I don't want you bringing the heat down on all of us and screwing up our play. Besides, wouldn't you rather get paid? This is business, right?"

Chaos looked from Joe to Tess and back to Joe. "You got a good-looking woman there, grifter. You want me to mind my business; then you should mind yours." He waved them off.

They slid out of the booth and walked out the back door into the gravel parking lot. The streetlights were on. An icy breeze cut across the lot. Empty beer bottles lay half-covered in the snow and torn plastic bags fluttered across the gravel. Three men wearing dark-colored parkas were huddled in the service entryway smoking marijuana. One of them glanced at Joe and Tess. Joe cocked the pistol in his pocket. "Hey, baby," the man said, "you looking for some company?" He motioned with his hand to indicate his friends and himself. "What's it cost to hook up a threesome? We're all gentlemen."

Tess moved up next to Joe's left side and put her arm through his. Joe brought his pistol out of his right coat pocket and turned it so that it caught the light from the street lamp. "Lady's busy."

The man took the joint offered by his friend with one hand and raised up his other hand. "Whoa, no disrespect, my man. Just looking for some action."

Joe nodded and slipped the cocked pistol back into his pocket. Tess squeezed his hand. She whispered, "Let's keep moving."

Joe spoke out of the side of his mouth. "Asshole called you a whore."

"You going to kill all three of them?"

"Don't know that I'd have to kill all three."

"Baby, let it go. This is Jonny's house. And we've got business."

The breeze stopped and snow began to fall; heavy flakes drifted slowly to the gravel. The man passed the joint and looked over at them again. "Everything okay?"

Joe didn't reply. He turned his back to the three men in the entryway. He let go of Tess's hand and put his arm around her. They headed for the Explorer, which was parked on the street. "You're better than that."

"I know it, baby."

"You're everything."

She kissed his cheek. "I love you."

"I love you."

When they'd gotten back in the Explorer and turned on the heat, Joe took out his phone and called Brandon. "You better get out of town for a few days."

"I was planning on moving. I just have to pack my apartment."

"You own anything as valuable as your life? Get out of town."

He hung up, turned to Tess, and shook his head. "Idiot."

"Think Chaos took the bait?" she asked.

"He won't miss an opportunity to squeeze. It's in his nature. He'll put his thumb on Franklin in the blink of an eye. With any luck, that'll provide the pressure to loosen him up. In the meantime, let's see what we can rake off the table."

They drove to Angie's apartment, the snow gently falling, the windshield wipers whapping back and forth, the road wet with melting snow. They parked in the visitor parking for the building next to hers and walked over. The parking lot and sidewalk were well lit. A young woman bundled up in a hooded down parka and walking a tiny black dog dressed in a green plaid sweater passed them on the sidewalk. "Hello," she said. The tiny dog sniffed at them. They nodded but said nothing.

They sauntered down the sidewalk until they saw the woman disappear around the corner of the building. Angie's car wasn't in her parking space. Her apartment was dark inside. They looked in the front windows, but they couldn't see anything. Joe picked the lock. They stood just inside the front door and put throwaway booties on over their shoes. Joe lowered the blinds in the living room and kitchen and then turned on the lights before he started searching. He found a black handbag hanging on a hook in the front closet. He took the cash and credit cards and tossed the handbag out onto the carpeting. Tess went back to the bedroom. She could hear the muffled sound of the TV in the apartment next door. The blinds were already down, so she turned on the lights. The cloth-covered jewelry box on the mirrored dresser contained nothing but costume jewelry and a pair of diamond earrings. She took the earrings and dumped the jewelry box out on the bed. She ran her arm under the mattress, looked under the bed, rummaged through the dresser. Lots of pretty underwear but nothing of value. The bathroom contained the usual collection of creams, contact lens solution, body washes, and shampoos. She looked in the bedroom closet almost as an afterthought. Sweaters on the shelf. Dresses and casual clothes on hangers. Safe sitting on the floor. She couldn't believe her eyes. She got down on her knees, put her hands on one side of the safe, and gave it a push. It was definitely bolted to the floor. She got Joe.

He laughed and rubbed his hands together when he saw it. "I love these cheap, third-rate safes." He had it open in a few minutes. Inside were rubber-banded bundles of bills — hundreds and twenties — $40,000 in total, and a notebook listing amounts added on particular dates. He sat on the floor looking up at Tess with the bundles in his lap. "Looks like he's banking at Angie's."

"Hiding money from his wife."

"Dates in the notebook are all recent and close together."

"There's got to be more to come," Tess said.

"Looks like it, doesn't it? How about we put the money back in the safe—make it look like we broke into the apartment but couldn't crack it?"

"Increases his confidence in the safe. He keeps adding to the pile and we come back for it after we get the fifty thousand."

"And if he doesn't add anything, we take the forty."

"It's worth the risk. If he could be banking somewhere else, he would. And this pile could get bigger fast."

"Much bigger. He's not spending this money." Joe put the money and notebook back into the safe.

In the kitchen, Tess found a loaf of whole wheat bread and a jar of natural peanut butter in an upper cabinet and a jar of organic grape jelly in the refrigerator. "You hungry?"

Joe shook his head. "You must be kidding. You know I don't like that healthy bread."

She made the sandwich right on the Formica countertop, piling the peanut butter on extra thick and wiping a thin layer of jelly onto the other slice of bread. "Fiber. It's good for you."

"Sticks between your teeth."

"I made it just the way you like it."

He sighed. "Give it here." He took a big bite out of the sandwich and set it down on the counter next to the loaf of bread, the jar of peanut butter and the jar of jelly. "Satisfied?"

"That wasn't so hard, was it? Let's get out of here." They left the lights on and the door unlocked.

Angie parked in her assigned space and got out of her Corolla. She didn't like leading the 8:00 p.m. intermediate yoga class. There were too many beginners and advanced students to keep the flow of the class going smoothly: one person needing extra help to do the basic pose, another wanting advice on how to make the pose more challenging, the real intermediate students getting confused by all the extra direction. She flipped her hood up, jammed her hands into the pockets of her parka and walked slowly across the parking lot, taking the shortest path to her apartment, watching carefully for icy patches. She'd fallen down on the sidewalk in front of her apartment the day before yesterday, and she still had a bruise on her hip. This winter was dragging on forever. She wiped her feet on the mat in front of her door.

The lights were on in her apartment. She thought she'd turned them off. She was going to have to be more careful. She put her key in the lock and opened her door. Her black handbag lay dumped out on the living room carpet. She took two steps into the room, shuddered, looked at the shelves over the TV— nothing missing—glanced across to the kitchen counter, took another step, saw the peanut butter jar and grape jelly jar and the sandwich with the bite out of it. Her eyes shifted to the hallway to her bedroom. She strained her ears, but she couldn't hear any voices or movement. All she could hear was the blood pounding in her head. She spun on her heels and ran out of the apartment, slamming the door behind her. She didn't stop running until she was in her car with the doors locked. She got out her phone. "Ronnie, Ronnie, somebody broke into my apartment."

"Hold on," Franklin said. "You caught me off guard. Your apartment's been broken into?"

"Yes, somebody's been in there, may still be in there—"

"Where are you?"

"In my car."

"Take a deep breath. Can you see your front door?"

"Yes. Ronnie, please, I need you."

"I know; I know. Have you got your coat on?"

"Uh-huh."

"Stay in your car. Watch the door. I'm on my way."

Franklin looked at his watch. Nine p.m. He got up from his desk in his home office, put his laptop to sleep and carried it with him. He stuck his head in the den, where Melanie was watching TV. "I have to go back to the office real quick to access a report that can't leave the building. I'll be back by ten."

Melanie looked back over the sofa. "Okay, honey. I might already be asleep by then."

"Have a good sleep."

"I love you."

"I love you, too."

Franklin got into his Volvo. As he backed out of his driveway, he was already trying to think of the quickest way to Angie's. If he cut through the neighborhood, it was twenty-five miles per hour, but there were only three stop signs and one light at the intersection with Ridgeview, which was a right turn. If he went down the boulevard, the speed limit was forty-five miles per hour, but this time of day the stoplights were out of sync. He decided to cut through the neighborhood. He took the first left onto Elmwood, pushed his car up to thirty-five miles an hour, looked both ways as he approached the first stop sign and rolled through. Somebody broke in? His mind was racing. Angie wasn't home. Must have been at work. Her schedule would be easy to check. Was his money gone? Was Angie involved? Was it the thieves that Samantha hired to steal Lilypad? How would they find Angie's apartment? Was it just coincidence?

An old yellow Buick was up in front of him, getting larger by the second. How fast was it going? Fifteen miles per hour? He was right behind it. He started to pull around, but headlights were coming. A black Ford blew past. The Buick came to a full stop at the second stop sign, waited and slowly pulled away. As it started to move, Franklin turned his wheel, stepped on the gas, and shot past the Buick in the intersection. He punched the gas, drove through the next intersection at thirty-five, and slowed almost to a complete stop at the stoplight before he turned onto Ridgeview. He could see the red roofs of Angie's apartment complex just up on the right. He had to quiet his mind. In a few minutes, he'd have some facts, some info; he could see for himself. He pulled into a visitor's space by the clubhouse and ran across the parking lot to Angie's car. She saw him coming and unlocked the door. He slid into the passenger's seat. She threw her arms around him. "Ronnie, I'm so scared."

"It's okay; it's okay." He rubbed her back through her down coat. He took her by the shoulders and looked her in the face. Her eyes were watery and bloodshot. "Did you see anyone leave?"

She shook her head. "No."

"They were probably already gone when you got home. Let's go have a look."

"Let's call the police."

"We don't want the police if we don't need them. We don't want to draw attention to ourselves. We'd have to explain why I'm here, and why you have a safe in a rental apartment. Let's just have a look. No heroics, just a peek."

"What if they're in there?"

"They're not in there."

"Are you sure?"

"I'm sure. We'll just have a peek."

"Okay."

They got out of the Corolla and walked casually up the sidewalk to the apartment, Franklin holding Angie's hand. The front door was slightly ajar. Franklin looked at Angie. She said, "It must have bounced when I slammed it."

Franklin pushed the door all the way open with his foot. He could see Angie's handbag upturned on the carpet and the jars of peanut butter and jelly out on the kitchen counter. "That's what you saw?"

She nodded.

"Nothing's changed?"

She looked around the room carefully. "No. I don't think so."

"Okay, let's have a look."

Franklin and Angie stood still in the middle of the living room in their coats, listening as hard as they could. The only sound was the furnace running. "Get out your phone," Franklin said. "No one's here, but just in case, be ready to dial 911."

They crept into the bedroom. Empty. The jewelry box was dumped out on the bed. Angie pawed through the earrings and bracelets lying on the comforter. "My good earrings. They're gone."

"Anything else?" Franklin asked. "Go look in your handbag."

Angie ran into the living room. Franklin opened the closet and got down on his hands and knees. The safe was locked. He put in the combination and opened it. He reached in, pulled out the bundles of cash, and flipped through them. All the money was still there. So if Samantha's thieves were the ones who broke in, they couldn't open the safe. Angie yelled from the living room. "My money and credit cards are gone."

Franklin closed the safe and met Angie in the living room. She was down on her knees going through her handbag. "Is that it?" he asked.

"Is that it? I'm broke and they've got my credit cards."

He got down on his knees next to her and put his hand on her shoulder. "I'll give you the money back. Report the credit cards as lost."

"But someone broke into my house."

"Your place isn't trashed. They couldn't get into the safe. They broke in when you weren't home. They did that on purpose. You're safe now. Think the cops will hang around here?" He kissed her gently. "I'll stay here with you until we're sure everything is okay." Her lower lip was quivering. "And I'll replace the earrings. It'll be like it never happened."

"Really?"

"Absolutely. Let's make sure all your windows and doors are locked." He helped her to her feet.

She was still frowning. "But what if they come back?"

"For what? They were probably crackheads. They took everything they wanted. Tomorrow they have to break in somewhere else. How do they know you didn't call the cops? They'll want to be at an apartment complex far away from here."

"Okay. We'll check the windows."

"Exactly. We'll check the windows and make sure everything is safe."

Melanie Franklin had pulled into the parking lot at the Ridgeview Apartments just in time to see Ronnie and Angie go into Angie's apartment and shut the door. She pulled into a parking space in the middle of the lot where she could watch Angie's door and put the BMW into park. Tears started down her face. She reached into her handbag for some tissues. As she dabbed her eyes, she started sobbing. She sat in her car crying, one hand on the steering wheel and the other pressing a wad of tissues against her eyes and nose. She'd been hoping, in her heart of hearts, that there was some innocent explanation for Ronnie's behavior, but here was proof positive staring her in the face. Her marriage really was over. She stopped crying, took a deep breath and blew her nose. She turned on her headlights, circled the parking lot to write down Angie's apartment number, and drove home. She felt a sudden urge to check their bank and stock accounts before she went to bed.

An hour later, Franklin was on his way home. He'd managed to convince Angie that the break-in was just a random event and that she was completely safe, even though he didn't believe it. She was safe; there was no doubt about that. She was safe because the break-in wasn't random. The thieves who stole Lilypad were involved with this somehow. They had called him demanding payment for the Leapfrog break-in, and now they were sending a message that they could mess with his life. Next step would be a blackmail demand. Pay us or we tell your wife about your girlfriend. So how little could he get away with paying them? Ten thousand? Fifteen thousand? Surely they weren't really expecting the full $50,000 they were promised. He could probably raid the Lilypad account for $15,000, but nothing more. Or maybe he could put the cops on them. He'd need Samantha's help for that. Just how would that work? He pulled into his driveway and pressed the garage remote button to open the door to the third garage. The house was dark. The light in the garage turned on as the door went up. Melanie's BMW and the old blue Toyota van that Kat drove were already in the garage. As he got out of his Volvo, two big men in gray parkas and ski masks ran into the garage. "Hey," Franklin said.

The first man swung wide and hit Franklin in the side of the head, knocking him into the side of his car. He dropped to his knees and tried to scramble back into the car, but the man grabbed his legs and dragged him back out. Franklin struggled and kicked, but the first man held him up from behind while the other man punched him repeatedly in the face and stomach. Then the first man let go of him and he fell to the concrete floor. His phone rang. The man in front of him kicked him in the face. The world went black.

When Franklin woke up, the garage door opener light was off and the men were gone. He was cold from lying on the garage floor. He stumbled over to the door to the kitchen in the dark, pressed the button to lower the garage door, and turned on the kitchen light. He went to the sink, turned on the cold tap, and scooped water onto his face. When he dried his face, he smeared blood on the dishtowel. He drank a glass of water and then went into the washroom to have a look at himself. His mouth was bloody and a knot was rising on his forehead. He unrolled a wad of toilet paper, wet it, and wiped at his face. Then he remembered the phone call. He fished his phone out of his pocket and went into his voice messages.

"The kid got thirty thousand from me; now the debt is yours. You pay or you're dead. Thirty thousand plus fifteen for the vig. Don't make me come for your family."

The phone went silent. Franklin looked up. Melanie was standing in the doorway in her flannel nightgown and robe. "My God, Ronnie. Where have you been? What happened to you?"

"Some guys jumped me outside the house. Must have followed me from the office. Downtown just isn't safe after dark anymore."

"You need to sit down." She guided him to a chair in the dining room. "You want a drink?"

"No, no, I should go to bed."

"Go to bed? You might have a concussion. You should go to the emergency room."

"I'll be fine. I just need some rest."

She crossed her arms and looked hard at his eyes. "You weren't at the office, were you?"

"What are you talking about?"

"Come, on, Ronnie, they have security. You weren't at the office. Where were you at?"

"Look, keep your voice down, you're going to wake up Kat. I don't want her to see me like this. I'm going to bed. I'll explain everything tomorrow."

Melanie watched him as he shuffled through the living room. He climbed the stairs one step at a time, using the handrail for support. She shook her head slowly. She'd been hoping to catch him with the smell of that other woman on him. Instead, she'd found this. Maybe he wasn't cheating on her, but he was definitely up to something he didn't want her to know about.

That's why he needed the night to get his story straight. After he disappeared up the stairs, she went to the pantry, got out a bottle of vodka, and poured two fingers into a water glass.

She stood at the kitchen sink looking out the window at the snow drifted up around the swimming pool and sipped her drink. She was glad she had checked the bank and stock account totals when she came home. All their money still seemed to be there, even though she hadn't been able to understand all the transfers that seemed to be taking place. She was going to have to keep an eye on him, scrutinize everything he said, watch everything he did, until she figured out what was really going on or until she couldn't stand it anymore. Either way, she wasn't going to be the clueless wife looking for a waitress job because her husband and the money were gone.

8: The Crucible

At 9:00 a.m. on Wednesday morning, Leroy Smalls sat in Stuart Jackson's office nodding his head at the appropriate times while Jackson yelled. "Have you seen these numbers?" Jackson stood up and tossed the *Wall Street Journal* down on his desk. "And the story that's being pushed on cable is even worse. The sharks are circling. The rumor, which is getting stronger by the day, is that Lilypad 5 is trash and we'll be bankrupt by the end of the year."

Jackson pulled his charcoal suit coat off and threw it at the chair in the corner behind his desk. "We're leaking like the dikes have been breeched. Someone on the inside is spreading misinformation. Right now I don't care about why. I care about how and I want it to stop. Your job is riding on this, Leroy." He sat back down, pulled off his glasses, and tossed them onto his desk. "Hell, who am I kidding? My job is riding on this. All of our jobs are riding on this. If the stock flushes, it won't matter if we get Lilypad out. It will belong to the company that takes over Leapfrog and fires us."

"I understand, sir."

"Do you?"

"I'm going to do whatever it takes."

"You sure about that?"

"You can mark this off your to-do list. Security is going to be so tight here that I'm going to know what people are thinking before they do. You've got my word, Stuart."

"Clean it up. If one of our competitors is behind this, I want to know who."

"Anything else?"

Jackson shook his head.

Smalls went back to his own office and printed out a list of all the personnel and their access to various levels of information. Only the senior staff could have leaked any information that was specific enough to be believable. And they had significant stock exposure. Still, he was going to have to get up Samantha's and Ronnie's assholes with a magnifying glass and tweezers. Two days ago, Ronnie had been willing to pay him $2,000 to not start a leak investigation. Why? He couldn't want the stock to fall; that was money out of his pocketbook. But he was obviously up to something. Before today, Smalls didn't care; Ronnie's secret business was just cash money to help pay his gambling debts, but now he had to know what Ronnie had gotten into. His own job was on the line. If the stock continued to fall, Stuart would certainly fire him first.

He slipped the printouts into a file folder and labeled it "priority research." And then there was Samantha. He wouldn't bother to look at her at all if she weren't working for Ronnie. She was squeaky clean. Except for that intern, Tess. She was flirting up Ronnie like he was the dream date to the prom. They build divorce courts because of women like her. He opened her file. Who the hell was she? Their personnel investigation of her had turned up the usual vanilla gravy: no felonies, reasonable credit report — she appeared to be who she appeared to be. But the trouble started right after she showed up. Sam broke her leg; Tess was wandering around here on her own; bad press went viral on the Internet. Could be coincidence. Tess shouldn't have been able to access anything important. But Stuart had outlawed coincidence until this leak was plugged and the leaker caught. Who was manning the front security counter today? Janie. He'd put her on digging into Samantha's and Ronnie's details. He'd take a look at Tess himself.

When Tess drove away at lunchtime in her beat-up red Civic, Smalls followed her out of the parking deck in his Crown Victoria. The day was sunny and cold. Lots of people were on the sidewalks, walking briskly with take-out sacks in their gloved hands or shuffling their feet to keep warm while they waited for friends outside of restaurants. Smalls followed two cars behind hers. She was a careful driver, no sudden moves, which made her easy to follow. At the corner of Orion and Fifteenth Streets, she pulled up at a Caffeination Coffee Shop. Smalls slid into the loading zone in front of Angelo's Italian Steak House. A man about fifty with salt and pepper hair and a moustache climbed in the passenger side of Tess's car and took a moment to kiss her before he put on his seat belt. When the traffic light changed to green, she pulled out into traffic. Smalls continued to follow.

Near the interstate and the old Lakeview Shopping Mall, Tess turned into the Green Valley Apartments, a rundown, red brick apartment complex. She parked next to a blue Ford Explorer. She and the middle-aged man got out and went into the end apartment. Smalls pulled into a parking space at the other end of the building. He wrote down the address of the apartment they went into and Tess's car license plate number. He lowered his window a few inches and lit a cigarette. Was she going to spend her whole lunch hour here?

He called a friend at the department of motor vehicles. "Hey, how they hanging? I got a car tag for you. Yeah, same money as last time." He read off the car license plate number. "Call me back." He flicked his cigarette ash out the window. Then he called a friend at the City Assessor's Office. "How are you, honey? You know who owns the Green Valley Apartments? Yeah, the dump out by the interstate. Can you find out who's renting a particular apartment? Great. Number 1211. Call me back. Cash is in the mail."

He finished smoking his cigarette and turned on the radio. A talk interview show was playing. He changed the station to pop music. His phone rang. "Yeah?"

"Mr. Smalls?"

"Yeah?"

"This is Thomas Raines with Longview Insurance."

"How can I help you?"

"I'm afraid there's no easy way to say this, but you can't borrow any more against your life insurance right now. You're at the limit."

"But I thought you said—"

"That was before I had a chance to look at the details of your policy. Sorry. I know this isn't what you wanted to hear. If I can do anything else for you, please give me a call."

Smalls set his phone down of the seat beside him. He had to get his hands on some money. Payday was almost two weeks away. He still hadn't sent his child support payment. If he could just get some seed money, he could win back enough to catch up his bills. He watched Tess come out of the apartment and drive away. A few minutes later, the middle-aged man came out and got into the blue Ford Explorer. Smalls followed the Explorer long enough to write down the license plate number.

Smalls detoured through the drive-through of a Wendy's on the way back to Leapfrog and ate a double cheeseburger and drank a Frosty at his desk while he waited for Samantha to return from lunch. When she hobbled by, he followed her into her office and closed the door. "Hey, Sam, I need to have a word."

She leaned her crutches against the wall and sat down behind her desk. "Closing the door. This must be ominous."

Smalls clasped his hands behind his back. "You just don't know. Stuart is wanting scalps. Your job is hanging by a thread." He nodded. "That's right." He pointed directly at her. "You've got this one chance to come clean. If I think for a moment that you're lying, I'm going to Stuart and you'll be escorted out of the building."

Samantha's mouth fell open. "What, exactly, are you talking about?"

Smalls sat down facing her. "You're going to tell me all about Tess and the man she runs with."

"What man?"

"Middle-aged, moustache, graying hair."

Samantha shook her head and shrugged as if she were entirely clueless. "I don't know any guy who's a friend of Tess's. Tess is an intern doing a job shadow—"

"Snap out of it. She's no techie. According to Carol, she can't do much more than file paper. Somebody's leaking info on the new program. Stuart is pissed. You've been acting strange."

Samantha took a deep breath. "If I tell you, you have to promise not to tell anyone."

Smalls nodded. "Finally. Now we're getting somewhere. If it's got nothing to do with the job, you've got my word."

Samantha looked past Smalls to the corner of the room. "Tess is my girlfriend. She needed the internship credit, so I brought her in here to help her out."

Smalls studied her face. "You expect me to believe you're a dyke?"

She looked him in the eye. "That kind of language is a violation of our discrimination policy."

"No offense, Sam, but I find it hard to believe you rate a woman that smoking hot."

"Everything isn't about looks. I expect you to believe the truth. And I expect you to keep your word."

Smalls kept studying her face. "So what about the guy I saw her with?"

"I've never seen him."

"Love can make you blind to things you ought to see. Maybe you're being played. Ever think about that? Tess ever around any confidential materials?"

"I'm not a fool, Leroy, or a child. Everything stays here in my office."

Smalls stood up. "I'm going to be watching you, Sam. And I want Tess out of here as soon as possible."

"By the end of the week."

"As soon as possible."

"The end of the week. That's only two more days. You're going to find out someone else is the leaker, Leroy, and then you're going to have to apologize."

"I've always liked you, Sam. I hope you're right. But I'll put you out the door if I have to."

It was midafternoon by the time Ronnie Franklin slipped into the office through the third floor door to the parking deck. The swelling had gone down on the purplish knot on his forehead. A piece of white tape stuck to his mustache covered the cut on his lip. His ribs still ached as he breathed, but he no longer limped when he walked. He sat down at his desk without taking off his coat. He scanned through his emails, looking for messages too important to ignore, hoping for good news from the Lilypad team. Nothing. Samantha hobbled into his office on her crutches. "I thought I heard you. Christ, what happened to you?"

"Fell down the basement stairs."

"Really? You look like you've taken up prizefighting." She closed his door. "Stuart's hot about our press coverage, so Leroy is investigating everyone."

"We just have to stay calm. Get rid of the potato man."

"You're just loving your euphemisms, aren't you? Did you change your mind about paying them?"

"I might find a way to give them a little something if it'll get rid of them."

"Want me to set up a meet?"

He shook his head. "Don't want to look anxious."

"Suit yourself."

"Anything on Lilypad?"

"The new code looks good, but we're not even close yet."

He nodded. "Well, I need to get something done here."

Samantha left the door open on her way out. Franklin checked his stock account. The automatic program had sold off his Leapfrog stock before the big drop. He'd cleared $562,000. He transferred the cash to his Cayman Island bank account. His plan was on course. He closed the browser he used for personal business and opened his Leapfrog browser. Under the New Development accounts, he noted that the flex account for incidental expenses contained $70,000. He figured he could siphon off maybe $10,000; make it look like Samantha or the team leader had ordered special equipment. Then he looked at the promotional account and the overtime account. All together he thought he could pull together $30,000 if he had to. But $30,000 wouldn't get those goons off his back. Who was the kid? Why did they give him $30,000 and why couldn't they get it back from him? Had the kid run off or was he dead? He cradled his head in his hands. The kid. The kid. Had to be connected to the Lilypad mess. What else could it be? The kid. Where was Sam's nephew, Brandon? Had he gotten himself into something that was biting back?

The door creaked. Franklin looked up and closed his browser at the same time. Stuart Jackson strode into the room and shut the door. His face was red and his hands shook as he spoke. "The rumors are true, aren't they?"

"What are you talking about, Stuart?"

Jackson took a step back. "What happened to you?"

"Long story. Fell down the basement stairs. Sit down. What rumors you talking about?"

Jackson paced in front of Franklin's desk. "That Lilypad is junk. It never would have been ready for the rollout."

"That's just bullshit, Stuart. Look at the progress reports. When we've had a chance to rebuild it, you'll see for yourself. It's going to be a big moneymaker for a long, long time."

"There's going to be a full investigation of the Lilypad program and the fire. If you sold off your stock before the price drop, you're gone. And if you had anything to do with the fire, you're going to jail."

"I don't know what brought this on, Stuart, but you're completely off base. You wait and see."

Jackson stormed out of Franklin's office, slamming the door behind him. Franklin looked at the door and took a deep breath. Stuart was a problem. He was overreacting to the media reports, losing perspective. Franklin needed to find a way to settle him down. If Stuart were thinking clearly, he'd know it was too late to investigate the fire. The crime scene had been cleaned up. And the hard drive had been melted in the electrical fire, so there was no way to find out about the quality of any programs on that server. Franklin could easily prove that he sold his stock because he needed the money, which wasn't a crime. It was his stock. He could sell it, throw it away, or give it away. It was nobody's business. If Stuart fired him, he'd just entangle Leapfrog in a wrongful dismissal lawsuit. Other than the inconvenience of having his name in the press and being temporarily unemployed, it was all gravy. He would make even more money off the lawsuit than if Stuart had left him alone.

Franklin smiled to himself and turned back to his computer. He might as well get some work done while he was here. He got a bottle of ibuprofen out of his desk drawer, washed down three with a glug from a bottle of water, and started studying the Lilypad team's latest work product.

A few hours later he was eating the last bite of a piece of pepperoni pizza from the Domino's around the corner from the office when his desk phone rang. He wiped the grease from his hands with a paper napkin and picked up the phone.

"You still owe us fifty thousand," the same man's voice said.

"I don't know what you're talking about."

"You want your wife to know about your girlfriend?"

"You're so predictable."

"Really? Have you decided how far I'll go to fuck up your life if I don't get the fifty grand?"

"Come on, we both know I don't have fifty thousand to give to you."

The man chuckled. "So what's your offer?"

"I might be able to scrape together twenty."

"You're a very funny guy."

"You're not the only one who wants money from me."

"But I'm at the front of the line."

"Think about the twenty." Franklin hung up. He felt giddy. He didn't know why, but the thieves didn't scare him at all. Maybe because Stuart's and the goons' threats seemed so much more real. He shook the crushed ice in his cup of Pepsi and sucked on the straw. Tell his wife on him. What a joke. The goons had threatened to kill him and Stuart had threatened him with jail. The goons were the ones he had to worry about. And if he wanted to pay them—God knows why he inherited the $30,000 plus the $15,000 in interest—he needed to get Stuart off his back so he'd have free rein to squeeze the money out of the project accounts. He set down his Pepsi and went back to work.

The next time Franklin looked at his watch, it was 10:00 p.m. He carried his pizza trash out of his office, locked his door, dumped the trash into the hallway trashcan, and pushed out of the glass fire door to the parking deck. There were only a few cars left in the third level, and none that appeared to belong to Leapfrog employees. As he unlocked his car, he noticed Jackson walking across the deck with his suit coat on and his briefcase tucked under one arm. He yelled, "Stuart." Jackson turned. Franklin waved, and then hurried over. "Stuart. So I wasn't the only one burning the midnight oil."

"What is it?"

106

"I just wanted you to know I understand the pressure you're under from the board of directors. We're putting the time in. The team is making great progress. I was just going over their work. No promises, but right now I'd say we're going to have Lilypad reassembled and good to go ahead of schedule."

Jackson nodded. "I'm still having you and Samantha and everyone working in New Development investigated. Anyone who's not shiny clean is going out."

"But how can you find any real evidence? The server was destroyed in the fire."

"Leroy still has it. We're getting some experts in to see if it's possible to pull any data off it. The people we've been in contact with — ex-NSA — say they can often pull fifty to seventy percent of the data off a computer that looks completely shot. That should be enough data to tell us if Lilypad was up to speed." He glanced toward his Mercedes at the end of the row. "I've got to go."

Franklin put his hand on Jackson's shoulder. "You're making a mistake."

Jackson knocked his hand away. He pointed his finger at Franklin's chest. "Mistake? If I find out you had anything to do with this fiasco, I'm going to ruin you." Jackson turned and started to walk away.

Franklin's mind went blank. He jumped on Jackson's back and grabbed him by the throat. Jackson staggered and dropped his briefcase. "You're fucking crazy." He clawed at Franklin's hands, wheeled around, and banged Franklin against a support post. Franklin let go and fell to the concrete.

Jackson ran for his car, digging in his pants pocket for the remote door opener. Franklin charged after him and tackled him. Jackson's head banged against the concrete deck. Jackson put his hands up into Franklin's face, trying to push him away. Franklin knocked Jackson's hands away and grabbed his throat with both hands. They rolled over, Jackson punching at Franklin's face, trying to make him let go, but Franklin dug his thumbs into Jackson's throat, increasing the pressure. Finally, Jackson managed to knee Franklin in the groin. Once, twice, three times. Franklin gasped and lost his grip. Jackson started to crawl away, but Franklin sprang on to him, grabbed him by the hair on his head, and banged his head against the pavement, over and over, until he stopped moving.

Franklin sat on top of Jackson, looking down into his open eyes. "My God, my God," he muttered. He put his fingers on Jackson's neck to check for a pulse. He was dead.

Franklin looked around furtively. How had this happened? The parking deck was eerily quiet. What time was it? 10:20 p.m. The security guard would be on his rounds in forty minutes. Fucking Jackson. Why couldn't he leave well enough alone? Franklin's hands were shaking. What could he do? He had to get out of here. He needed to make this look like a mugging. He picked Jackson up under the arms, dragged him to his car, and flipped him over face down like he'd been attacked from behind. There was a bloody patch welling up on the back of Jackson's head. Christ. Franklin looked at his own hands and the front of his coat. No blood. Thank God.

He scurried back and forth over the area they had run across until he found Jackson's car keys and briefcase. He put the keys into Jackson's hand and set the briefcase by the car door as if Jackson were just getting into the car when he was struck from behind. He dug Jackson's wallet out of his jacket pocket. There — instant mugging. He looked around to see if he'd left anything incriminating.

His phone vibrated. Message from Angie, wondering where he was. She was his alibi. He had to get over to her apartment. He started to put his phone away. What was he missing? The message from the goon. Wait a minute. He could use that old TeleArc beta program they'd developed for the Feds to transfer the voice message. TeleArc hadn't lived up to expectations, but it could easily do that. He glanced at his watch. 10:35. He still had twenty-five minutes. He fished Jackson's phone out of Jackson's front pants pocket and rushed to his Volvo. He sat down in the passenger's seat, cabled both phones to his laptop, and used his wireless to access the main server in the building. He input his password. Incorrect. God, no. The PDA he kept all the passwords on was in his office.

Okay, okay, think it through. He tried another password. Incorrect. 10:45. He took a deep breath, and then counted off the numbers and letters with his fingers. This had to be it. He input the password. Bingo. He scanned down through the folders on the main server, found "government applications," scanned down the list—what had they called the TeleArc project? TelephoneTwo. There it was. He opened the program. Easy as pie. He transferred the goon's message from his phone onto Jackson's voice mail. Two birds with one stone. The cops wouldn't look any further than the goons. That'd pay them back for kicking him around. He ran back to Jackson's body and put the phone back in his pants pocket. 10:55. Oh, no. He scanned the deck as he hurried back to his car. No time left. He couldn't be seen leaving. He lay down in his backseat and waited. At 11:05 he heard the security guard's footsteps and saw his flashlight beam cut across a nearby pillar. Franklin's heart was pounding in his chest. He could barely breathe. But the guard didn't stop. The sound of his steps receded in the distance. Franklin peeked out the backseat window. The security guard was gone. How had he missed seeing Jackson? Had he just looked in the wrong direction at the right time? Franklin chuckled to himself. He couldn't have been any luckier. He climbed into the front seat and drove out of the parking deck through the far side exit.

Leroy Smalls got a call from Steve Barnes, the on-duty security guard, at 2:00 a.m. When he arrived at the State-To-State Insurance Company Building at 2:30 a.m., the police were already there. Yellow tape cordoned off the area around Stuart Jackson's car. A sheet covered Jackson's body. Two detectives stood nearby directing several uniformed officers. Smalls half smiled. Gonzalez and Meyers. What shit creek were they up to be called out at this time of day? Smalls lifted the yellow tape and stooped under it. "Marty, James," he called out.

Detective Gonzalez turned. He was forty-two years old with short gray hair and an athletic build. A jagged scar ran down his right cheek from a childhood accident. He wore a tan overcoat over a brown suit, blue shirt, and matching pattern tie. "Hey, hey," he called back. He turned to his partner. "Jimmy, you remember Leroy?"

Detective Meyers nodded. He was thirty-five years old. His muddy blond hair was thin on top but covered his collar at the back of his neck. He wore khakis, a red golf shirt, and a wrinkled blue blazer. His teeth looked like flat pebbles floating in his mouth. When Smalls reached them, Meyers slapped him on the shoulder. "So this is where you landed?"

"On both feet, brother. At least until today," Smalls said.

"Your guy called it in."

"Where is he?"

"One of the uniforms is sitting with him in the lobby. He identified the victim. Stuart Jackson."

Smalls squatted by the body and lifted the corner of the sheet. "Damn. That's him. I was hoping the kid was wrong."

Detective Gonzalez called over to a uniformed officer. "Rickman, when the ambulance comes he's ready for transport."

Detective Meyers motioned with an outstretched arm. "Techs will wait until daylight to finish going over the scene."

"Sure," Smalls replied.

"We've got some questions."

"Let's go into my office. I'll put on some coffee."

Smalls used his keys to let them into the third floor entrance from the parking deck. "I need to call the chairman of the board and the management team. Have you called Stuart's wife?"

"Let's get some info first."

"Okay."

They sat around Small's desk enjoying the warmth. Detective Gonzalez leaned back in his chair and sipped his coffee. "Life of Riley. How long have you been here?"

"Right off the job. Five years. This is the first bad thing that's happened."

"Really?"

"Come on, this is a technology company. As long as no one's taking the equipment home to sell on eBay or trying to sell the secrets, I'm just the guard dog in the front yard."

"Nine to five."

"Nine to five with an hour for lunch."

"So what's on your plate right now?"

"I've been investigating security breaches."

"About what?"

"We were supposed to roll out a new product, but we had a fire in the server room, so the rollout had to be postponed. There's been rumors in the financial press. The stock price dropped."

Gonzalez nodded. "So what did Jackson want you to do?"

"Stuart was mainly concerned with the stock price. He wanted the fire investigated to make sure it was an accident, and he wanted to know if anyone was leaking info to the press. He wanted leaks plugged. He wanted to know who the leaker was; wanted to know if anyone broke into our offices and if they stole anything."

"What have you got?"

"Nothing, really. Sniffing around usually stops leaks, at least temporarily, so that was my focus." Smalls drank from his coffee. "Have you got an angle?"

"Don't know. Later today the techs will fill us in, but a robbery gone bad is hard to buy."

Smalls nodded. "Jackson was a tough competitor, but he was a good man. Anything you need, just let me know."

"Thanks, Leroy."

Gonzalez glanced at Meyers. "Let's get back to it."

They all stood up. Smalls said, "You don't need my guy anymore, do you? I'd like to send him home."

"We've got his statement, so, yeah, cut him loose. Tell him we'll be in touch just to go over everything."

Smalls walked the detectives to the third-floor door. Then he rode the elevator down to the lobby. Steve Barnes, a skinny black kid too small for the army, sat behind the security counter all alone. The police had left. Barnes looked up from the surveillance screens. "Mr. Smalls."

"Hey, Steve," Smalls said. He came around the back of the counter and patted Barnes on the shoulder. "How are you holding up?"

"I'm okay."

"First time you ever seen a dead guy?"

He nodded.

"You did good. Played it by the book. The cops will probably interview you again, just in case you remember something, but they'll wait until all the evidence is processed. You go on home.

We'll pay the rest of your shift. You can see a counselor on your insurance, which I want to encourage you to do."

"Okay. Thanks, Mr. Smalls. Shame about Mr. Jackson."

"Yeah, it sure is."

Barnes pulled on his work parka and left out the front door. Smalls locked up behind him. He sat down behind the counter, sighed, and looked at the computer monitor. What a cluster fuck. The last thing he needed was cops digging around. Even guys he knew. Who knew what they might find? Something on the computer monitor attracted his attention. What was he looking at? He smiled. Barnes had been watching the live feed on the security camera of the cops working the crime scene in the parking deck. It was just like watching a fuzzy TV show.

Wait a minute. What was on the security camera footage? Smalls scanned back through the recording until he saw an indistinct figure attack another indistinct figure who must have been Jackson. The time/date stamp indicated that it was seven minutes after 10:00 p.m. The resolution was too grainy to identify the attacker. Smalls watched the killer drag Jackson out of the frame and then come back a few minutes later and get into Ronnie Franklin's car.

He paused the recording. Ronnie Franklin? It just wasn't possible. He wasn't a killer. Smalls looked up from the computer monitor. Outside, the wind was gusting and it had started to snow again, big fat flakes falling rapidly. But Ronnie and Sam were up to some foolishness that Ronnie was willing to pay him $2,000 to ignore. And Sam had something going with Tess, who had something going with mustache guy. The person who killed Stuart was too tall to be Tess. Sam had a cast on her leg. But mustache guy? He was the right height. Smalls tapped a blank DVD on the edge of the desk. What were they all up to? Maybe they were all in the clear. Or maybe they would pay to keep the police out of their business. It didn't matter if they were innocent. All that mattered was what the security footage showed.

Smalls put the blank DVD into the DVD drive on the computer and copied the recording of Jackson's murder. He knew what he was supposed to do: put Jackson's murder first, give the DVD to Gonzalez and Meyers, and let the chips fall where they may. But what could the DVD potentially be worth? Ten thousand? Thirty thousand? A hundred thousand? With that kind of money he could pay off all his debts. Start over. He got out a marker and wrote "Ronnie" on the DVD. It would be a shame to give up the chance to make that money if the DVD were no help finding Jackson's killer. He put the DVD into a case, and then put it into his coat pocket. He studied the recording on the computer screen. How far could he go? Gonzalez and Meyers would pull the recording first thing in the morning. It had to show the murder. He tapped his finger on the counter and rubbed his chin. He smiled. But it didn't have to show the killer getting into Ronnie's car. He erased that part of the murder from the hard drive and copied in some empty frames from an earlier day to fill out the recording. With the grainy resolution and poor lighting on the recording, someone would have to be looking pretty hard for tampering to figure out what he'd done. That would give him at least a couple of days to chase down the leads himself and figure out what he was going to do with the full DVD — sell it or give it to Gonzalez and Meyers. They'd be angry with him, but if they needed the DVD to make their case, they'd accept whatever excuse he told them.

9: The Squeeze

At 7:00 a.m. on Thursday, Joe and Tess climbed into the back-seat of Samantha's Camry. They were bundled up in their heavy coats. Most of the Pay-U-Save Grocery Store parking lot was empty, but the near end by the café was parked full. "Okay," Joe said, "why did you need to see us so early?"

Samantha turned in the front seat to look back at them. She put her arm up on the seatback. "Stuart Jackson was murdered in the State-to-State parking deck last night."

Joe and Tess nodded. "It was on the morning news," Tess said.

"It's a bad break for us. Attracts attention but doesn't pay us any money," Joe continued. "On the other hand, it does create a certain amount of distraction."

"You're serious?"

Joe shrugged. "I don't believe it was a mugging, but that's neither here nor there. We didn't have anything to do with it, so the evidence will lead away from us."

"Well, Leroy is onto you two."

"What do you mean?"

"He came to my office, threatened to have me fired, said he knew Tess didn't have any technical skill. He wanted to know who you were. He'd seen you two together."

"What did you tell him?"

"I said Tess was my girlfriend and I didn't have any idea who you were."

Tess laughed. "Very smart, Sam."

"He said you've got to the end of the week, though I don't know what Leroy will want now."

"So that's today and tomorrow," Joe said.

"What are you going to do?"

He shrugged. "You want to get rid of us? Put fifty thousand in our hands. We were looking for a new way to put the pressure on Franklin. Maybe the murder will make him finally want to pay us off to get rid of us." He opened the car door. "See you later."

"Are you crazy? You've got to get out of here."

"See you at work," Tess said.

Samantha watched them get into the Explorer and drive away. It was as if she'd woken up in some sort of bizarre alternate reality. Stuart murdered, the police investigating. It gave her the chills. Joe and Tess couldn't possibly believe what they were telling her—that it would just keep everyone distracted. Leroy was suspicious. He was like a dog with a bone. And now anything he found out would go directly to the police. She needed to talk with Ronnie. He had to listen to reason. The server was destroyed. The programmers in the Lilypad work group were rewriting the code without making so much as a peep about how bad the original program was. Joe and Tess were the only weak link left in her and Ronnie's alibis. They needed to pay them off and get them out of the picture. Today. The sooner the better.

By midmorning Detectives Gonzalez and Meyers were back at Leapfrog Technologies. The crime scene crew had completed its work in the parking deck. The yellow tape was gone, the blood had been scrubbed up, and the parking deck was open. The parking deck security camera footage was too grainy to be of much use, but the police now knew that Jackson had fought for his life. There was bruising around his throat. Fiber and skin were embedded under his fingernails. The cause of death was blunt force trauma to the back of his head. If he'd carried a wallet, it was gone, though his pants pockets contained money, house keys, and a cell phone. Those were the facts. Chances were that someone Jackson knew had killed him. So they had to turn his life upside down. And since Jackson was killed at work, the best place to start was at his work.

"Will this do?" Smalls held open the door to the fifth floor conference room. He'd lain in bed for three hours and hadn't slept for most of that. His eyes were bloodshot and his face was stubbled with a beard, but he was dressed in his usual blazer and tie. "There's good cell reception in here. Plenty of table space. Restroom right down the hall."

"Thanks, Leroy; this will work fine," Gonzalez said. He glanced at his clipboard. "Can you send Ronnie Franklin to us?"

Gonzalez and Meyers were seated on the far side of the Formica-topped conference table, yellow pads in front of them and the audio recorder ready to go, when Franklin came into the room. He wore a black turtleneck shirt and faded jeans. The cut on his lip was still visible through his beard and the bump on his head was a greenish-purple bruise.

"Mr. Franklin, please sit down. I'm Detective Gonzalez and this is Detective Meyers. We're trying to gather information about Mr. Jackson's movements yesterday."

"Anything I can do," Franklin said. "This whole thing is completely crazy. Stuart murdered in the parking deck." He shook his head.

"Did you meet with Mr. Jackson yesterday?"

"Yes. It was about 5:00 p.m. He stopped by my office."

"What did you meet about?"

"The Lilypad rollout—the data-mining program."

"It being delayed?"

"Yeah, and the leaks and the financial press killing the stock. The odd behavior of my second-in-command."

"Who's that?"

"Samantha Bartel."

"How odd?"

"Hey, this rollout is a big deal. Make or break for all of us. Sam's one of those people who show their nerves."

"You look like you've been in a fight."

"Fell down my basement stairs day before yesterday. Really hurt. Probably should have gone to the emergency room like my wife wanted. Didn't get into the office until late yesterday, which is why I was still here at seven. Manager at the Domino's Pizza teased me about it yesterday evening when I went over to pick up some take-out."

"Where were you between nine p.m. and two a.m.?"

He looked from Gonzalez to Meyers and back again. He bit his lower lip. "I know I need to be straight with you two, but I'd rather my wife didn't know. She thinks I was here, but I was at my girlfriend's."

"After you fell down the stairs?"

"Everything isn't about sex."

"Name, address, phone number." Gonzalez pushed a piece of paper and a pencil across to Franklin, who wrote down Angie's information.

"Anything else I can do for you?" Franklin asked.

"Was Mr. Jackson concerned about anything out of the ordinary? Did he seem preoccupied?"

Franklin shook his head. "Stuart was completely focused on his job—trying to get Lilypad out as soon as possible. The fire in the computer room—that was unusual, but the fire marshal's report said it was an accident." Franklin shrugged. "I didn't know anything about Stuart's personal life. He didn't talk about it and I didn't ask."

"Thanks for your time."

Franklin pushed his chair back and stood up. "Do you think you're going to catch the killer?"

"We're going to do everything we can."

"Good luck."

The detectives watched Franklin leave the room. Meyers turned off the audio recorder. "What do you think?"

"I think I want to know more about his accident. His face didn't get marked up falling down the stairs."

Meyers smiled. "Wife beat him up?"

Gonzalez chuckled. "Wouldn't be the first."

"Should he go on the list for a DNA sample?"

"Yeah," Gonzalez said, "just to be safe."

Meyers made a note on his pad.

"Okay, who's next?"

Samantha leaned into the threshold of Franklin's office and knocked on his open door. Her crutches caused her suit coat to ride up under her arms and the front of her shirt to pull loose from her skirt. Franklin looked up from his laptop. "Christ," she said. "Carol said you still looked bad, but you really do look like shit. How do you feel?"

"I must feel better than I look; I came in to work."

She hobbled into his office, sat down, and leaned her crutches within easy reach. "What's up with the police in the conference room?"

"They're trying to track Stuart's movements. It's less of an inconvenience for us than everyone having to go to the police station."

"Have you seen the team's work product from yesterday? They're finally making some headway."

"Yeah, looks like we might be turning the corner. Say, where's your nephew, Brandon?"

"I haven't seen him since Sunday. He resigned. He could be halfway to California by now."

Franklin got up and closed his office door. "Some goons jumped me on Tuesday night."

Samantha's eyes were wide. "What? Like gangsters?"

Franklin nodded. "Got me when I was going in my house, if you can imagine that. I got a phone message that said the kid was gone and I had to pay his debt. Only thing I can think of is Brandon owes some goons some money."

Samantha pointed at Franklin's bruised face. "So that's their work?"

"Oh, yeah."

"I'm sorry, Ronnie. I thought Brandon leaving was for the best. One less loose end. I don't know anything about him owing anyone money. What are you going to do?"

Franklin shrugged. "This is a business expense, so I'm trying to find the money in the open accounts — you know, advertising, overtime, etcetera." He waved his hands in the air like a conductor leading an orchestra.

"You don't think those gangsters had anything to do with Stuart's death?"

"Don't know."

"Stuart didn't tell you anything or hint at any kind of problem —"

Franklin shook his head. "It does help us, though."

"How's that? Stuart's dead, the stock is in free fall as we speak, and there's a police investigation."

"All true. But the board is going to stay out of the way until the cops are finished, so no one will be looking at the actual value of the Lilypad program, which means we have even more time to get it right. We've just got to keep our people on task."

"All my assets except for my condo are tied up in Leapfrog stock, so I'm in worse shape now than I was last week. If we can't make Lilypad right, I'm screwed."

"You didn't sell? Hang tight. The stock will shoot back up after the board picks a new CEO."

"Are you insane? If you sold a lot of your stock before the drop, the cops will be all over you."

"Sammy, if you could only see your face. You need to relax. Trust me; the stock I sold won't be an issue. The only thing I'm worried about is putting together the money to pay off those goons."

Samantha glanced at the closed door. "What about the thieves? If the cops get on to them, we're in big trouble. We need to pay them off."

"The cops aren't going to find out about them. It's not going to happen. Don't worry about it. I've got everything under control."

Samantha pulled herself up onto her crutches and hobbled out of Franklin's office. Something was up with him. He seemed — what? More confident, more sure of himself. He was certain their plan was going to work. She wished she felt that certainty. All she saw was Ronnie's usual hubris. Stuart dead. The police investigating. Gangsters after Ronnie. It seemed they were adding to their problems, not resolving them.

But maybe Ronnie was right. Maybe this was the kind of situation that he really understood. With Stuart out of the way, Ronnie would have a lot more leeway to scrape together the money to pay off the gangsters — whoever they were — and Joe and Tess. Maybe that was it. Maybe he was just going to move some money around, make it look like someone else had spent it, and hope the amounts would be too trivial to notice after they fixed Lilypad and the cash started rolling in. But if that was his plan, she needed to make sure that the money trail didn't point to her.

As she was hobbling toward her office, Detective Meyers stuck his head out of the conference room. "Ms. Bartel."

"I'm on my way."

By the time Samantha got into the conference room, Meyers was already sitting next to Gonzalez on the other side of the conference table. She leaned her crutches against the table and shifted a chair sideways so that she could extend her casted leg.

"Okay?" Meyers asked. He turned on the audio recorder. Gonzalez looked across the table at Samantha. "I'm sure this is all a big shock."

Samantha nodded.

"Do you know anything about Mr. Jackson's movements yesterday?"

"I know he was in the office."

"But you didn't see him?"

"No. I'm not getting around very well yet, so I'm sticking to my desk pretty much. Stuart didn't call me or stop by my office, so I didn't see him. Although I did hear him in the hall when he went to see Ronnie."

"Mr. Franklin?"

She nodded.

"You have to speak for the recorder."

"Sorry. Yes."

"What time was that?"

"Must have been close to five, because I went home at five-thirty."

"When did you break your leg?"

"On Saturday. Fell in the stairwell at the mall."

Gonzalez shook his head. "You people and your stairs. You fall down some stairs at the mall, and Mr. Franklin falls down the stairs at his house. Where were you treated?"

"Mercy."

"Care if we see the record of your treatment?"

"No. Knock yourself out. Paramedics treated me at the scene. Took me to Mercy."

Meyer's cell phone rang. He answered it. After he hung up, he turned to Gonzalez. "Techs are all finished. They sent off the

DNA. There's a message on his phone they think we should hear."

"You all done with me?" Samantha asked.

"Almost," Gonzalez said. He looked through his notes. "I understand you've been under a lot of pressure lately with the problems surrounding your new product rollout?"

"Who said that?"

"So it's true."

"We've all been under a lot of pressure. A lot is riding on this new product."

"Where were you between nine p.m. and two a.m.?"

"Home in bed."

"By yourself?"

"Yeah, I live alone."

Leroy Smalls sat in his Crown Victoria at a red light at the intersection of Lakeview Mall Road and Orion Drive. Half a MacDonald's coffee sat in his cup holder. He yawned and rubbed his eyes. Stuart murdered. Ronnie's car on the security camera. And Ronnie didn't fall down the stairs. He got his ass whipped. Probably didn't even know how to put up a fight. The light changed to green. Smalls drove another block and turned left into the Green Valley Apartments. The blue Explorer was parked down near the end apartment, which was rented to Joseph Campbell. Joe and Tess, Tess and Sam, Sam and Ronnie. If Sam and Ronnie were doing dirt, it wouldn't be against the company. They both got their bonuses in stock.

And if Sam were telling the truth about her relationship with Tess, then all the dirt fell on Tess and Joe—her husband, her lover, whatever. Assuming that Stuart was killed over something having to do with Leapfrog. As Smalls crept down the parking lot, Joe came out of the apartment, got into the Explorer and drove away. Was Campbell a hard guy? Hard enough to kill a man? Smalls followed him back down Orion Drive into the business district south of Orion College. Joe pulled into a metered on-street parking spot in front of a Caffeination Coffee Shop and climbed out. Smalls double-parked beside him, jumped out of his Crown Victoria without putting his coat on, pointed at Joe and shouted. "Hey, you, I want to talk to you."

121

Joe looked over his shoulder. Smalls caught up to him on the sidewalk. "Do I know you?" Joe asked.

Smalls poked his finger into Joe's chest. "I know you. You got yourself hooked up with a murder at Leapfrog Technologies."

"Stop poking me. You're talking crazy. You must have me confused with somebody else." Joe turned to walk away.

Smalls grabbed his shoulder. "You're dirty. I can smell it on you."

Joe turned back toward him and knocked his hand away. There was menace in his eye. "Step away from me."

"You think you can walk away from this one? I got you on video."

"You're insane." Joe walked into the coffee shop.

Smalls got back in his car. Campbell had the reflexes of a man who'd fought in a prison yard. And he was definitely big enough to be the guy on the video and strong enough to kill Stuart with his hands. A white Nissan Sentra stopped behind Smalls and honked. Smalls raised up a hand in acknowledgement and put the Crown Victoria into drive. Maybe Campbell had Ronnie's car, using it as cover to do what? Who knew? Stealing equipment, stealing ideas? Who cared? Stuart left late, saw him, they tussled, Campbell killed him. It was almost too simple, but that's the way it often was. Push the first domino. One thing led to another. Next thing you knew you had a murder scene. Ronnie? There was no way he did it. He didn't have the stones. Smalls smiled to himself. But the DVD showed what it showed, and if Ronnie didn't want to go to trial, well, he was going to have to pay.

Samantha shut her office door, leaned her crutches against the wall, and sat down behind her desk. Only one person could have told the cops that she was under a lot of pressure: Ronnie. And what did "under a lot of pressure" mean? It meant "unstable." Ronnie never missed a trick. Every way that he could he was setting her up to take the fall just in case any evidence turned up on the melted server. She was the unstable one, the one who needed the money, the one who had dealt with the thieves, the one who had involved her nephew. He had deniability on the server fire. She really wouldn't be in the clear until Lilypad was fixed and flying off the shelves. And then Ronnie would take all the credit.

She swiveled her chair and looked out the window at the red brick office building across the street. What could she do? If the company went bankrupt, her stock would be worthless. And she'd never get another job in the industry. Nobody hires a middle-aged loser. Maybe there was a way she could turn the tables on Ronnie. Get him to pay off Joe and Tess. With the thieves and Brandon gone, there would be no direct evidence against her. Ronnie was the one who sold his stock just ahead of the price drop. Ronnie was the one in control of the accounts the payoffs came from. She sighed. Who was she kidding? Tess and Joe knew how to do that sort of thing, but it just wasn't in her skill set. She was just dreaming. She swiveled back to her desk, put on her computer glasses, opened her laptop, and looked in her emails.

Later that morning, there was a knock on her door. "Come in."

Tess came in. She was wearing brown cowgirl boots, a tan skirt with an Indian beadwork belt, and a pink flower print shirt that was open to reveal her cleavage.

"That outfit is a little much for the office, don't you think?"

Tess shut the door. "Just channeling the ditsy girlfriend." She sat down and crossed her legs. "Anything new?"

"Cops interviewed me."

"Of course."

"Asked me where I was last night."

"And they found out that you're a sad, lonely woman living all by yourself in your empty condo."

"You're not funny."

"You didn't do anything. The cops are looking for evidence that leads to a murderer. They're not just randomly investigating everything. They have lives and new cases coming in."

"They think it might be connected to the Lilypad problem."

"Why?"

"They asked me if I was under a lot of pressure because of the delay in the product rollout."

Tess took a deep breath. "Honey, you're just talking paranoid now."

"Yeah? Well, when I'm arrested is when you're going to run."

"Keep your voice down. We're going to be gone soon enough."

Samantha leaned over the desk. "Ronnie told me this morning that he sold his stock before the price went into free fall. Guess where the police are going to focus if they find that out?"

"I bet the money isn't in his checking account. Besides, the cops would need a warrant to look at his financials. Did we tell you we found his girlfriend?"

"Girlfriend?"

Tess nodded. "I bet he has a second set of accounts somewhere."

"He's got an old PDA that he still keeps all his passwords on."

"Really?"

"I know. It's not very safe, but he didn't want his passwords on a company device."

"He carrying that?"

"No, his smartphone keeps his appointments. He leaves the PDA in his office."

"So," Tess said, "are we going to work together on this?"

Samantha stalled for a minute, not sure if she wanted to take the step from sabotage for a good cause to straight-up theft. "So you're talking about raiding his accounts?"

Tess nodded. "He owes us fifty thousand. Of course, if you've got another way for us to get our money and get gone, I'm happy to hear it. Besides, he's been stealing your ideas and taking the credit how long?"

"I've just—I've just never done anything like this before."

"You want payback or you want to be a doormat? He's not going to give you respect; you've got to take it."

"You're right; you're right," Samantha said.

Tess reached across the desk and patted Samantha's hand. "Of course I'm right."

"So what are you going to do?"

"Is Franklin in the building?"

"No, he had to go meet with the board of directors."

"I'm going to get that PDA."

Tess peeked out into the hall. The hall was empty. The door to the conference room was open and she could hear talking, but she couldn't hear what was being said. Franklin's door was closed and, no doubt, locked. She reached into her handbag, put her hand on her lock picks, and stepped out into the hall. Just as she got to Franklin's door, Carol came up the steps from the third floor carrying a pile of files. "Hey, Tess."

Tess shoved the lock picks back into her handbag. "Hey."

"What you got there?"

Tess smiled sheepishly. "Good luck charm."

Carol motioned with her head toward Franklin's door. "I think he's off-site until after lunch."

"Really? He asked me to stop by to see him."

The phone rang in Franklin's office. "See? Nobody home. Have you got a few minutes to give me a hand?"

"Sure."

"Just let me drop off these files." She took the files into the conference room. Tess put her hand on the snow globe in her handbag. Carol reappeared. "Good luck charm, uh?" They walked back toward the stairs.

"I know it's silly, but it's one of those kid things. Gives me confidence."

"What is it?"

Tess pulled the snow globe from her handbag, flipped it upside down, and then righted it. The snow fell on a beach scene with a Ferris wheel and mermaid. "Atlantic City" was written across the bottom of the globe. "My dad brought it back for me when I was eight or nine. I used it for a demonstration speech in the fifth grade. After that, it's always been my good luck. Pretty lame, huh?"

"Surprising it still has water in it."

"See? Good luck."

An hour later, everyone cleared out for lunch. Tess went back upstairs. Samantha was in her office with the door open. "No lunch for you?"

"I brought some carrots and celery. Want some?"

"You hear about my detour?"

"Yeah. Carrying a snow globe. That's new."

"Why don't you come out in the hall and play lookout?"

Samantha grabbed her crutches and gimped out into the hall. Tess nodded toward the stairwell. "The bell on the elevator will guard the other side."

As Samantha moved toward the stairs, Tess found the lock picks in her bag. She glanced toward Samantha, who nodded. Tess picked the lock on Franklin's door, and then opened it. She sat behind Franklin's desk and tried the top drawer. It was locked this time. She pulled the file drawer all the way out. Nothing stashed behind the files. The second drawer still contained the vodka bottle, but the extra smartphone was missing. She jimmied the top drawer with a jeweler's screwdriver. Inside the drawer was a jumble of office supplies. She pulled the drawer out and set it on the desktop. In the back right corner was an old PDA. She turned it on. The password screen came up. Shit. She put the PDA into her bag, slipped the drawer back into the desk and relocked it, set the chair where it had been, and locked the office door on her way out. Samantha was already hobbling down the hall. They went into Samantha's office. Samantha closed the door. "Well?"

Tess held the PDA up in her hand. "I've got it."

"Got it? What if he looks for it?"

"It's password protected."

Samantha sighed. "Give it to me. I'll figure out the password and look for the financial accounts and passwords."

"Make it quick. Give me a call when you have them."

"We have to do the transactions from his computer."

"His computer? Why?"

"So if anyone traces back where the accounts were accessed from, they find Ronnie's computer."

"Okay," Tess nodded. "Find the accounts and passwords. We'll start planning the next step."

Detectives Meyers and Gonzalez, bareheaded even though their overcoats were buttoned up, were on either side of Jonny Chaos, walking him to their unmarked police car, a white Chevy Impala. They were pulling him along a little faster than he wanted to go, his black leather coat flapping open and his shoes dragging on the sidewalk. Chaos's hands were cuffed behind his back, throwing his chest out and stretching the fabric of his shirt across his belly. He looked back over his shoulder at Bobby and Little Tom, who stood outside the door to the Green Swan Bar and Grill, watching, black stocking caps on their shaved heads and their hands in the pockets of their insulated work coats, unable to do anything since they couldn't use violence. "Call Southmore," Chaos yelled.

Bobby pulled a cell phone from the pocket of his worn jeans, hit the speed dial, and held the phone up to his unshaven face.

Detective Meyers put his hand on the top of Chaos's head to direct Chaos down into the backseat. "Enjoy the ride."

"You guys won't keep me two hours."

The detectives climbed into the front, Gonzalez driving. "We'll keep you long enough." Meyers read Chaos his rights.

They drove in silence to the police station, where they took Chaos down the hallway to the interview rooms, a dark, windowless corridor that smelled of cheap floor cleaner, and unlocked the door to room number two. In the middle of the room a steel table was bolted to the floor. One metal chair, with arm restraints hanging from its arms, sat behind the table, while two steel-framed chairs with plastic seats and backs sat in front of it. They put Chaos in the chair behind the table and cuffed him to a steel ring welded to the tabletop. "You look good, Jonny," Detective Gonzalez said. "The only way we could improve your appearance would be changing that black leather for a prison-issued jumpsuit."

"Fuck you."

"You know Stuart Jackson?"

"Never heard of him."

"He was beat to death in a parking lot last night."

"My condolences."

Meyers sat down across from Chaos and held up a cell phone. "Mr. Jackson's phone. What kind of messages do you think he has since you don't know him?"

Chaos slouched back in his chair. "It's been so long since you guys harassed me that I'd forgotten how stupid and obvious you are. When I say I don't know a guy, I don't know him."

Meyers turned on the phone, went into the voice messages, and clicked on a particular message. Chaos's voice said, "The kid got thirty thousand from me; now the debt is yours. You pay or you're dead. Thirty thousand plus fifteen for the vig. Don't make me come for your family."

Chaos sat up in his chair. "That's been tampered with. I never met that guy. I never called his phone. I never left a message."

"Come on, Jonny," Gonzalez said. "Jackson inherited a debt and told you to fuck yourself. You sent your boys to tune him up and they got carried away. It's clear as day."

"Clear as mud. Where's my lawyer?"

"You make a statement now, we might be able to get you some rhythm. We know you don't kill people who owe you money."

Chaos looked up at the security camera in the corner of the ceiling. "Lawyer."

Gonzalez and Meyers left the room. The door bolt slid home. Chaos looked at his wrists, the cuffs chaining him to the steel ring in the center of the table, the metal cold and hard, and wondered how his voice got off Franklin's phone and onto Jackson's. Had to be some sort of technology trick, which meant there had to be some way to show the message had been moved.

And who moved it? Franklin thinking he could avoid paying? Was he that stupid? Probably. Computer nerds always thought nobody else was smart enough to figure out their bull-shit. Chaos shifted his weight, trying to make himself more comfortable. What he knew for sure was that Joe Campbell put him onto Franklin. So this was Campbell's fault. He should have taxed him the moment he laid eyes on him. Him and his woman. What was Campbell's angle? How was he making money out of this? Chaos hooked his ankles around the legs of his chair and scooted his chair toward the table. As soon at Southmore got him out of here, he was going to put his guys on Campbell. Nobody worked in this town for free. He was going to keep the pressure on Campbell until he had all the money he was due.

Leroy Smalls stood in the doorway to Franklin's office. It was three thirty in the afternoon, there were bags under his eyes and his face was chalky gray, but his blazer and slacks were as crisp as they had been at eight in the morning. Franklin looked up from his laptop. "Leroy, how can I help you?"

Smalls smiled, walked into the office and shut the door behind him. "Well, Ronnie, you know how it is around here."

Franklin shrugged. "There's a lot going on with the murder investigation and rebuilding Lilypad, but what exactly do you mean?"

Smalls sat down. "I bet your meeting with the board of directors this morning went really well. I bet they were sharing the love."

"They did want me to step up around here until they find a replacement for Stuart."

"You wanting Stuart's job?"

Franklin shook his head. "I'm a technical guy. That's out of my league."

"But you do want to keep your job?"

"Where you going with this, Leroy?"

"I've got the only complete copy of the security footage from the parking deck camera."

The color drained from Franklin's face. "The parking deck video?"

"That's right. And what do you think it shows?"

Franklin shook his head.

"It shows a shadowy figure getting into your car and driving away from the scene. I'll tell you for free that if I thought you'd killed Stuart, the cops would have the footage right now."

"Okay, let me explain—"

"I don't need an explanation. One hundred thousand buys the DVD."

"Are you crazy? Where can I get a hundred thousand? I'd be better off taking my chances with the cops."

"You're made to fit for this one, Ronnie. Don't underestimate what a jury can convince itself of. They start out seeing shadows, they look fifteen times and a little old lady believes she can see the scratch on your chin."

"I can't get a hundred thousand. I've got my family to think of. I've got to have college money."

Smalls nodded. "What can you get?"

"I might be able to put together thirty thousand. I could probably scrape together that much."

"Now you're just talking silly. I just might take seventy thousand for your freedom, but thirty, no way."

"I can get fifty if I dip into Kat's college money, but that's it."

"Fifty thousand?"

"Yeah. Fifty thousand, but it'll take me a few days to pull the money together."

"You give me the money, I give you the DVD, and we're done. No more favors; no more looking the other way."

"Jesus, Leroy, you're pulling my teeth here. I thought we were friends."

"It's not my car on the DVD." Smalls stood up. "Day after tomorrow at the latest. You don't want to fuck with me."

"Okay. I'll get the money. Day after tomorrow."

Franklin watched Smalls leave his office. The video cameras. Stuart had installed them after the parking deck vandalism. Shadowy figure getting into his car. He could explain that. He didn't need to pay. His car was missing. He hadn't noticed. He left it in the parking deck. Didn't know it was gone, except he drove it to the board meeting this morning. So that wouldn't work. What else could the police get besides his car? He threw away the clothes he was wearing. And the shoes. So what could they find? He sold his Leapfrog shares. That's it. But if the cops focused on Leapfrog, they could find the money missing that he'd taken for the down payment to pay the thieves. Then the melted server could come up for another look. Sam was set up to take the blame, but she'd implicate him as soon as the cops knocked on her door. She'd turn on the thieves as well, and they'd say anything to avoid jail; that's what criminals did. Still, they couldn't implicate him directly. With Samantha it would be "he said, she said." So he could probably win in court, but what would a criminal lawyer cost? It was all about the video. How grainy was it? Could it be enhanced? If the images could be blown up, he was fried. He couldn't take that chance. He

130

couldn't go to jail. Fucking Stuart Jackson. It was all his fault. If he had minded his own business, not been in such a hurry to lord it over everyone, they never would have had to sabotage the server.

Franklin looked down at his laptop. Leroy was a greedy bastard. Fifty thousand. Leroy thought he had him by the short hairs, but there was no way he was giving him that money. Maybe he could kill him? But how, where? Leroy would be on his guard. He was an ex-cop. He carried a gun. Franklin didn't know anyone who was reliable for that sort of job. Besides, he'd just be trading one blackmailer for another. He opened his desk drawer to get his PDA, but he remembered the password on the Cayman account, shut the drawer and opened the browser on his laptop. There it was: $562,000. The house was worth more than that, but it was mortgaged and he wouldn't be able to keep the house if he ran. He'd have to let Melanie have it. Or maybe she could sell the house and join him later. There had to be a couple hundred thousand in equity. They could home-school Kat. Get their relationship back on track. Lots of possibilities. Then there was the $40,000 in the safe at Angie's. He looked at his watch: 4:30 p.m. She'd be at work. He could swing by for the money on his way to the airport. If she was there, he could ask her to go with him. All he had to do was buy a plane ticket to the Grand Caymans. He logged out of the Cayman account page and opened Kayak. Then he stopped. No reason to leave any incriminating evidence on the computer. He could buy a ticket at the airport. He deleted his browsing history.

Franklin went down the stairwell to the third floor with his briefcase in one hand. Carol was behind her desk at reception. "Home so early?" she asked.

"Early supper, then back to the salt mine." He held up the briefcase.

"See you tomorrow."

He tossed his briefcase into the back seat, started the Volvo, and backed out of his spot. Should he go home for clothes? What would he take? Shorts, t-shirts, summer suit, swimming trunks. What would he tell Melanie or Kat? Last-minute business trip. Was he crazy? He didn't need to take any chances.

Airport. Screw the clothes; screw the safe. Good thing he kept his passport at the office.

Smalls followed Franklin out of the parking deck, keeping half a block behind in his Crown Victoria. The sky was clear with a few wispy clouds. There was still an hour of daylight and rush hour was just beginning to ramp up, so there were enough cars to hide his Crown Vic, but not so many as to keep him from watching Ronnie's Volvo. Smalls lit a cigarette and lowered his window enough to knock the ash off. Ronnie drove through the intersection with Chandler Street, which was the last straightforward route to Clareview Heights, so he wasn't going straight home. He turned on Ridgeview. Smalls flicked his cigarette butt out the window. Gym or girlfriend? But Ronnie didn't turn into either driveway. If he took the next right, there was a 90 percent chance he was going to the airport. Could he actually be running? Smalls thought about speeding up, cutting Ronnie off or catching him in the airport parking lot, confronting him, talking him out of running, smacking some sense into the fool.

Ronnie took the right turn. Smalls pulled over on the shoulder of the road. Maybe he should just let Ronnie go. Stay out of it. Ronnie hadn't done anything to him and the $50,000 was gone. Cars whizzed by. Somebody honked. Smalls glanced into his rearview mirror. He'd have to find another way to get the seed money he needed. If Ronnie were arrested and started talking, the police and Leapfrog might find out about the $2,000 he'd taken from Ronnie to look the other way. He'd lose this cushy job. That's the last thing he needed. Smalls looked over his shoulder to judge when he could pull back out into traffic. A Toyota minivan was coming down the street. There was a gap behind it. He watched as it passed by him. Kept watching it as it — and the gap — moved on down toward the cars stopped at the intersection. He got out his phone and called police dispatch. "Patch me through to Detective Gonzalez."

"Hello?"

"Hey, Marty, this is Leroy. Ronnie Franklin is heading for the airport right now. Just made the turn onto Airport Road. I think he's running."

"Christ. You couldn't give me a little more warning?"

"I wasn't sure until a minute ago."

Gonzalez was quiet for a moment. "I'm sorry, Leroy. Thanks. I owe you one."

"And Marty, you're going to be pissed, but I've got a DVD for you."

Ronnie Franklin sat at a table in the AllStars sports bar in the airport, eating a half-pound burger with fried onions and barbeque sauce on it, and drinking his second draft beer. Most of the tables were full, but he'd managed to get a table with a good view of the big screen TV. Getting through security had been uneventful. The line had been short and the family of mom, dad, and two grade-school kids that had been three people ahead of him were seasoned travelers: empty pockets, no belts, slip-on shoes. There was still twenty minutes before boarding for his flight to Miami, where he would connect with his flight to the Caymans. Basketball highlights flashed by on the TV. Franklin took a bite of his burger, chewed, took a drink, swallowed. As he set the mug down, he heard a chair scrape. He turned his head as Detective Gonzalez, tan overcoat open over his brown suit, sat down.

"What a coincidence. Mind if I sit?"

Franklin shook his head. "Where are you off to?"

"Niece getting married tomorrow."

"Congratulations."

"Business trip?"

Franklin drank from his beer. "No, with all the pressure and craziness, I'm just taking a long weekend."

"Without your family?"

Franklin smiled a broken smile. "That's part of what I need a break from. Not blaming my wife. I can't claim to be the best husband in the world."

"Sorry to hear that, but I think you're going to have to change your plans."

Franklin looked over his right shoulder. Detective Meyers was standing there with his hands on his hips.

"Come on," Franklin said. "I made these plans before Stuart was killed."

"No, Mr. Franklin," Gonzalez said, "You paid full price today and you're traveling without bags. You're coming with us."

"Easy or hard," Meyers said.

"Let me pay my check." Franklin motioned to the server.

Mark Southmore, an overweight, pink-faced man who was starting on a severe, blond-gray comb-over, stood beside Jonny Chaos in the aisle between the desks in the police department squad room with his hands in the pockets of his expensive black suit. "If you need to see Mr. Chaos, call me for an appointment."

"If we need Jonny," Detective Meyers said, "we know where to find him."

"No travel," Detective Gonzalez said. "We may have more questions."

Southmore led Chaos out through the glass doors to the hallway. Meyers glanced back toward the holding cells. "So what do you think this is about?"

Gonzalez sat at his desk. "I'm not letting Jonny off the hook yet, but this is looking more and more like an office thing."

"What did Leroy have to say?"

Gonzalez took a DVD out of his sports coat pocket. "Take a look at this." He pushed the DVD into the slot on the side of his computer. Meyers pulled his chair over and sat down. They watched the grainy footage. An indistinct figure attacked another indistinct figure in the distance in the back corner of the picture.

"We've seen this," Meyers said. "It's off the security camera in the parking deck."

"Keep watching." The figure moved closer and got into a car. The car backed out. The license plate was clearly visible.

"What? Leroy clipped the footage he gave us? What the hell was that all about?"

"Who knows? Fed me a load about needing to check up on a few things for his bosses."

"Do we know whose car that is?"

"It's Franklin's. And if Franklin hadn't rabbited, Leroy would probably still be holding out on us."

"That's bullshit."

"If I hadn't worked with him on the job, he'd be back in a cell, too." Gonzalez motioned with his head toward the door to the interview rooms. "Let's see what we got."

They went back into the hallway to the interview rooms and unlocked the door to room number four. The room smelled of sweat and fear. Franklin was sitting in the metal chair on the far side of the table, his wrist cuffed to a steel ring on the tabletop. "Mr. Franklin," Gonzalez said, " how are you?"

"Why am I chained to the table? Where am I going to go?"

Meyers sat down facing Franklin. "Sometimes when people are scared, and they contemplate what they've done, they hurt themselves."

"I haven't done anything. Okay, I should have told you I was going to take a quick trip—"

Gonzalez slammed his fist down on the table. Franklin jumped in his seat. "Mr. Franklin, we've seen the security camera footage from the parking garage."

Franklin looked from Gonzalez to Meyers and back again. "What are you talking about?"

Meyers shook his head. "You killed Jackson; then you got in your car and drove away. It's all on the DVD."

"That's not possible. Somebody must have stolen my car."

"And brought it back?"

"To incriminate me."

Gonzalez glanced at Meyers. "Do you believe that?"

Meyers shook his head.

Franklin sputtered. "Why would I kill Stuart? It doesn't make sense."

Gonzalez looked Franklin in the eye. "Why don't you work on your story? We'll be back."

Gonzalez and Meyers went back out into the squad room. "So why would Franklin kill Jackson?" Gonzalez asked.

"Something to do with the computer program that was connected with the fire?"

"Jackson found out something."

"Maybe he just fired Franklin for being incompetent," Meyers said.

"So we need to pull Franklin's life apart. Hot tempered? Calculating? Over his head? What's his home life like? What's up with the girlfriend? We figure out his motivation and he's going to fold. He hasn't got the heart to brazen through to a trial."

"I hear you. What do we do with him in the meantime?"

"We've got enough to hold him. Put him in a cell. That should make his situation seem real enough."

Meyers glanced back toward the interview rooms. "Suspect locked up in twenty-four hours. It must be a record. You want to get a drink?"

Gonzalez shook his head. "I should go home. I already missed dinner and I'm supposed to help Tim with his math homework."

"Then why don't you get out of here, Marty? I'll hand Franklin over to booking."

"See you later, Mom." Kat went out the kitchen door to the garage of the Franklins' house wearing her dance team uniform. She carried her navy wool coat under her arm.

Melanie Franklin looked up from the dishwasher, where she was making the final adjustments to fit a saucepan into the bottom rack. "The roads are icy, honey. Be careful." She shut the dishwasher and turned it on. The machine made a low hum and began filling with water. Melanie turned to the hand wash. She was scrubbing off a cookie sheet when the phone rang. It was a number she didn't know. She picked up the phone without taking off her yellow rubber gloves.

"Melanie," Franklin said.

"Where are you? You didn't answer when I called. You've missed dinner."

"Listen, honey," Franklin said, "I only have a few minutes. You remember Stuart was murdered?"

"Yeah."

"The cops arrested me. They just now let me use the phone."

"They arrested you?"

"I need a lawyer."

"You're in jail?"

"Yes. I'm in jail. Find me a lawyer. This is all a crazy misunderstanding."

"Why?" She sat down at the dining room table. "Why do they think you did it?"

"I don't know. Find me a lawyer. Ask your friend Sally. Her husband is a lawyer."

"Family law." Melanie noticed that her yellow glove had made a wet spot on the walnut tabletop. She wiped it dry with her apron.

"But I bet he knows somebody. Somebody good."

"How we going to pay them?"

"Pay them?"

"They'll want a retainer."

"So?"

Melanie looked through the doorway from the dining room to the living room. A fire burned in the gas fireplace. "We don't have any money. I still can't believe you're in jail."

"The bars are real enough. Use the checking account."

"We need that money for bills we can't pay with the credit cards. Why don't you get a public defender?"

"We make too much money. Besides, I want a real lawyer, not a plea-bargainer."

"We can't use the checking account. There's not enough there." The line was quiet for a moment.

Franklin sighed. "I sold some stock, remember?"

"I thought that was all reinvested."

"Not yet. The timing wasn't right. Go online to Cayman Island Bank." He gave her the username and password.

"I got it."

"The money's there, honey. Get me out of here."

Melanie hung up the phone. She felt slightly dizzy. She walked back into the kitchen, got out a pad of paper and a pencil, and wrote down the username and password before she forgot it. Then she rinsed off the cookie sheet and set it in the drying rack. Cayman Island Bank. She squeezed out the sponge and wiped off the granite counters. She'd never heard of that bank before. How much stock had he sold? How much money was in that account? Were there other accounts she didn't know about? What had Ronnie gotten involved in?

She set the sponge down next to the cold-water tap, draped the rubber gloves over the edge of the sink, and hung the apron up in the pantry. The first thing she was going to do was have a look at that account and move all the money somewhere else. Then, if there was still time, she'd call Sally. She didn't want to call too late in the evening. She sat down at the computer desk in the kitchen and held her head in her hands. She wasn't going to cry anymore. Ronnie in jail. Did he realize how embarrassing this was for her and Kat? He could stew in his own juices overnight. He'd been keeping secrets: the girl at the apartment, the fight he'd been in, and now the hidden bank account. Did she even want to hire a lawyer for him? Maybe she should be hiring one for herself.

Joe and Tess parked in the spot under the streetlight in front of their run-down, red brick apartment building. The wind during the day had blown a micro-snowdrift across their sidewalk and there was one set of footprints through it. Joe turned off the headlights. "So, on the one hand, Samantha's paranoid that she's going to be arrested and, on the other hand, she's helping us rip off Ronnie Franklin."

"That's about the size of it. There's no logic to it, but there you go."

"You took his PDA, and she's going to break the password."

"Yeah."

"Honey, you are a bad, bad influence."

She smiled. "Thank you."

"So let's review the money. We got the fifty thousand before the break-in. We know Franklin has around forty in the safe at the girlfriend's. We picked up some pocket change there. Now we got a chance to clean him out."

"We have to share with Samantha."

"We'll see how that goes."

She pecked him on the cheek. "I love it when you talk dirty."

"Don't get carried away. We have to be out of here by tomorrow evening or find a way to deal with Smalls."

They got out of the Explorer and started up the sidewalk. Joe had his keys in his gloved left hand, and his right arm linked with Tess's. She hadn't bothered to zip up her parka and was holding it closed. The heels of her cowgirl boots clicked on the sidewalk as she walked. "Hurry up," she said. "I'm freezing."

"Hey, Campbell."

Joe and Tess turned. Chaos's thugs, canvas work coats and watch caps, their black gloved hands already squeezed into fists, were moving toward them fast. Joe felt for the automatic pistol in his coat pocket, thought better of it, and let go. He handed the house keys to Tess. "Keep moving," he said to her. She went up the steps, opened the storm door, and unlocked the front door. Then she turned with her hand on the knob and watched. Joe sized them up: the tall one hulking over him—silver tooth, neck tattoo, dead man's glare; the other one shorter and heavier with rat's eyes and a tiny red goatee. "I remember you guys. You work for Jonny."

Rat Eyes sniggered. "You're a smart guy. Boss said you were a smart guy."

Silver Tooth gave Joe a push. "The boss doesn't like being jerked around by the cops on account of some asshole working his own game. You said Franklin was good for the thirty grand. Well, the cops got him, so the boss says you owe the thirty."

"The cops got Franklin?"

"Uh-huh. And you're carrying the thirty plus the fifteen."

"That's bullshit."

Silver Tooth gave him another push.

"It's still bullshit."

Rat Eyes punched him in the side of the head. He bent sideways with the blow and then stood back up. "Let's get this over with."

"You're not going to run?" Silver Tooth said.

"Would running help?"

Silver Tooth swung at him. He put his arms up in front of his face. Rat Eyes punched him hard in the stomach. He folded over and sat down on the snow piled by the walkway. Silver Tooth gave him a nudge with his heavy boot. "Pay attention. You're paying. Next time we won't play nice. Might find your sweet piece at home while you're out. So beg, borrow, or steal. Just so you pay us first."

"Two days. Give me two days."

Silver Tooth pointed down at him. "Two days. That's your whole life if you don't make this right." He nodded at Rat Eyes.

They walked across the parking lot and got into an old Dodge truck.

Joe got up and dusted the snow off his parka. Tess still stood between the storm door and the front door. "You okay?"

"Yeah."

"Where's your gun?"

"In my pocket."

She watched the truck drive away. "They're gone."

They went into the apartment. Tess switched on the wall light. "Your face looks okay."

"Come on, you know as well as I do they weren't trying too hard. It's just business. They knew they didn't have to convince me that they were serious, just like they knew I had to complain. You want a drink?"

He didn't wait for her to answer. He went into the kitchen, got down two short glasses, put ice into them, and poured in three fingers of scotch. When he turned with the glasses in his hands, she was standing next to him. She took one glass, stood up on her toes to kiss him on the lips, and went into the living room to sit on the black leather sofa. He followed her. They sat for a little while, drinking, looking at the blank screen of the TV. She kicked off her boots and put her feet up on the coffee table. "So the cops got Franklin?"

"Whatever that means. Jonny Chaos is our number one problem. Two days from now we're going to be gone. Serves me right for using Brandon's debt to pressure Franklin. Call Samantha."

Tess got out her phone. "Hey, Sam. Sorry to call so late. I didn't wake you, did I? It's been a busy day. You get the password?"

"Yeah. I copied all the info we need," Samantha replied.

"So we're on for tomorrow?"

"Unless Ronnie finds out his PDA is missing."

"We heard a rumor that Ronnie was arrested."

"Arrested? The police think Ronnie murdered Stuart?" Samantha asked.

"Who knows? But if he stays in jail, that gives us a little more time."

"If the cops are this close, maybe we should skip the whole thing."

"Samantha. This was your idea. You need the money. We need the money. All we have to do is reach over and take it. It's just lying there on the table. Turn on the computer. Move the mouse around. Five minutes tops. Did you find some other pile of money today?"

"No. I just don't want to go to jail. If it's too dangerous—"

"Sam. Start thinking with your head. This is easy money."

"Then let's do it tomorrow or not at all."

"It's tomorrow, then. See you at work." Tess hung up. She turned to Joe. "Did you hear?"

"Yeah." He squeezed her hand. "Nice work there. She's about to pop. And we've worn out our welcome here. Let's get our stuff together tonight, so we can get out of here as soon as we've transferred Ronnie's cash."

"Let me finish my drink first."

"Sure, baby. It's been a long day. Finish your drink."

10: Last Chances

The next morning, Friday, Samantha sat in her office reading the progress reports from the Lilypad team on her laptop. The last section of code they'd rewritten was a major improvement. It was all based on the original work. Ronnie had been right. They'd just needed more time. If the other two sections went this quickly, they wouldn't need six months. And now she was in charge. She'd get the credit if she could complete the rewrite before Stuart and Ronnie were replaced. Stuart—what a shame. He'd been a good leader, even if he was obsessed with the stock price. And Ronnie—the cops were crazy to think he'd killed Stuart. They'd figure it out eventually. He'd land on his feet. It was a shame that this was the only way she was going to get a chance to shine. She was just finishing her notes when Leroy Smalls knocked on her door. "Come on in, Leroy."

Leroy shuffled in and plopped down in the chair opposite her. "I'm already tired and it's not even lunchtime. I hear congratulations are in order."

"I don't know about that. It's just a lot of extra work on top of my usual job and it's temporary, until the board of directors finds a manager to run this place."

"Still, it shows that the board has a lot of confidence."

Samantha closed her laptop. "What's up?"

"I talked with a friend over at Lakeview Mall security. He said the security cameras show that you were chasing a guy with red hair dressed all in black when you had your accident. I'm guessing Fred Olsen."

Samantha nodded. "You're right. There was a leak in the office. We all knew it. I thought maybe Ronnie was involved, so

142

I was afraid to tell anyone. I was trying to sort it out on my own."

"With your girlfriend?"

"I didn't want to go alone."

Smalls rubbed his chin. "So did you find the leak?"

"I broke my leg."

"But you thought Fred Olsen was involved?"

"Thought he could be."

"And that's the story you're sticking with? That you and Ronnie and Tess and Joe Campbell aren't doing some dirt? Just keep repeating it until you believe it."

"Leroy, I don't have the slightest idea what you're talking about."

Smalls smiled. He got up, walked to the door, and turned. "Pretty crazy about Ronnie, huh? Never would have made him for a killer. It's the kind of thing makes you wonder what people are capable of. Did you know I've still got the burned-up server; that Stuart had contacted some computer forensics people? You get in bed with the devil; you might wake up in hell." He walked away before Samantha could reply.

Samantha looked out her open office door. It hadn't taken Leroy any effort at all to contradict her original story. As long as the computer fire remained an accident, she'd be in the clear. The board of directors was relying on her to reassemble Lily-pad. They wouldn't fire her based on a theory and circumstantial evidence. They would want facts. But would a forensics analysis of the melted hard drive provide those facts? Leroy was too good at his job for her to just wait and hope he didn't discover the truth. The safest thing to do would be to finish destroying the server. Where was Leroy storing it? How could she find out? Maybe she could get Tess and Joe to help her.

Smalls found Tess in the copier room, where she was helping Carol produce information packets for the emergency board of directors' meeting. Twelve dark green folders lay out on the worktable with twelve piles of paper lying face down next to each of them. The copier clacked and flashed as the pages copied and rolled out onto the copy machine tray. Smalls looked at Carol's desk, saw she was on the phone, and closed the copier room door behind himself. Sam, Tess, Ronnie, and Joe Campbell were definitely partnered up on some sort of shady deal. Sam had turned out to be a much better liar than he thought she would be, but that wouldn't save her in the end. Tess wasn't her lesbian lover. She was just a straight-up crook.

Smalls nodded his head. This was his last chance to get the seed money he needed to turn his financial situation around and he was going to push hard. Tess looked up from the worktable, a stack of freshly copied papers in her hands. She was wearing a tan dress that buttoned up the front, black tights, and a red and blue scarf wound loosely around her neck.

"You're looking good," Smalls said.

Tess set the papers down and put one hand on her hip. "Excuse me?"

"Hey, sugar, you and Samantha better get your story straight."

"What are you talking about?"

"She says you're her gay lover. I think that's all bullshit. I think you and your partner—Joe Campbell—are players. I think you all had something to do with Stuart's death."

"That's crazy."

"Maybe. But you're going to pay me ten thousand dollars to keep my suspicions to myself."

"You're extorting me?"

Smalls came up close to her. "That's right. You got a problem? Let's take it to the cops. They're right here in the building." He grabbed her wrist.

"I think you better let go of me."

Smalls pushed her back against the table and rubbed up against her. "I think you better talk to your partner and get me my money. Today. I know where you live and I know what you drive." He bent down and kissed her neck. She pushed him away. "Don't tell me you're new at this, 'cause I won't believe it." He stepped back and smoothed his regimental striped necktie. "Cat got your tongue? I don't care what your game is, girl; you got to pay to play." He left the copier room door open on his way out.

144

Tess wiped the side of her dress where he'd pressed against her. Smalls was trying to push his way to the inside of their game, but he didn't have a clue. She made a fist to stop her hand from shaking. Ten thousand dollars. Joe would negotiate that down if he felt like they had to pay. She shook out her hands and took a deep breath. Everything was okay. This wasn't Seanboro. She wasn't locked in a storeroom waiting to take a beating; she could escape anytime. She picked up the papers she'd set on the worktable and distributed them among the twelve piles. The copier finished making the last copy. The room was deathly quiet. Tess picked up the papers in the copier tray. Carol stuck her head in the door, her computer glasses hanging from a chain around her neck. "Tess, the detectives are ready to talk with you."

"Thanks. I'll head right up."

Tess distributed the last set of papers onto the twelve piles. She didn't have any intention of going to the fifth floor conference room. She looked out the door to the copier room. Carol was away from her desk. Tess walked nonchalantly through the reception area and out the door to the third floor parking deck.

A few minutes later, Meyers came down to the reception area in his shirtsleeves, the cuffs of his blue shirt turned up. He glanced into the copy room and then scratched the back of his head. "Hey," he said, turning to Carol, "you haven't seen Ms. Campbell?"

Carol turned from her computer monitor. "I thought she'd gone up to see you. Maybe she went to the restroom."

Meyers went back up to the fifth floor and down the hall to Samantha's office. "Ms. Bartel, have you seen Tess Campbell? We're ready to interview her."

Samantha looked over the top of her laptop. "Can't find her? It's Friday. Maybe she's gone to class. She'll be back later. After lunch I think."

"But the rest of your staff are here?"

"In the cubicles downstairs."

"Great. We were hoping to finish up today."

Tess parked her beat-up Civic next to Joe's Explorer in front of their apartment building, unlocked the door to their apartment, and went inside. "Joe," she called out. She heard the toilet flush. She shrugged out of her coat and laid it over the back of a living room chair. Joe appeared in the hall.

"Thank God I caught you," she said.

"What's up?"

"Your phone is turned off."

He took his phone out of his pants pocket. "Sorry. It was on vibrate." He sat on the arm of the sofa and looked at her expectantly.

"Smalls is shaking us down."

"It's never surprising, is it? What does he want?"

"He wants ten thousand."

"Everyone wants to get paid, but nobody wants to work. What does he know?"

She told him what happened in the copier room.

He took both her hands in his. "I ought to kill him just for touching you." He let go of her hands, walked to the window, and looked across the parking lot. "You know, he's going to keep digging until he breaks Samantha." He turned to look at Tess. "She just called me. He's got computer forensics experts coming to look at the burned-up server."

"Will they find anything?"

"I don't know. We've got to get something on him. What do we know?"

"He's divorced, has kids, needs money."

"He has a pension and a job. It's not drugs. What does that leave?"

"What if there's nothing on him? What if he's just a greedy asshole?"

"If he breaks Samantha, ex-cop or not, we'll have to put him in the trunk of a car and put the car in a lake. Of course, it would be easier, and safer, to kill Samantha. Cops wouldn't waste much time looking for her killer."

"Kill her after we get Franklin's money? That seems a little harsh, baby."

"I'm just brainstorming, honey. Who knows? We might have to pay Smalls. Chaos we can outrun. Maybe that's the way with Smalls, too. We get Franklin's money today, and we slip away, dump the cars. By the time Smalls has the goods on Samantha, or the cops find Brandon, for that matter, we'll have new names." He looked at Tess. "What do you think?"

"I think that we've got to be careful. Sam's jittery. If the cops really have evidence against Franklin, you know he's going to lie and deal. He's got no choice. He can't do the time."

Joe laughed. "This is a death penalty state. To get life, he's going to have to say we knew he was going after Jackson."

"Right now, we could walk away, buy ourselves a few more hours' head start."

"Let's stick with the plan. Today's our last day. We connect with Samantha, have a look in Franklin's accounts, and then it's hasta la vista."

"Okay." Tess nodded. "The cops want to interview me."

"Sure. They're interviewing everyone. Your story will stand up for a day. No problem. Go back to the office. Check in with Samantha. Tell her we'll meet at five thirty at Franklin's office."

Ronnie Franklin stood at the pay phone in the concrete block hallway of the city jail. He wore an orange jumpsuit with the legs and the sleeves rolled up. He was unshaven. He hadn't been able to go to sleep on the thin, vinyl-covered mattress in his cell, and all he'd had for breakfast was rubbery white bread toast and weak coffee. "Melanie?"

"Ronnie," she said. "How are you?"

"Have you hired a lawyer yet?"

"I'm working on it, but I'm not so sure it's such a good allocation of resources."

"Melanie, this place is a nightmare."

"But when they realize you're innocent, they'll let you out. If we hire a lawyer, that money is gone."

"Did you look at the Cayman Island bank account?"

"Yes, I did. I looked at it last night."

"So you know there's plenty of money."

"But how long will it last if you lose your job?"

"Lose my job?"

"You were on the TV this morning. They said you were arrested at the airport trying to flee."

"All the pressure at work. I just had to get away for a few days."

"Without telling me?"

"Melanie, darling, please hire the lawyer."

"What if there's a miscarriage of justice, and they keep you in jail? What will we live on? What will pay for Kat's college?"

"Please, please, please hire the lawyer."

"I'm thinking about it." She paused. "You know, Ronnie, I didn't know anything about the Cayman Island bank account. Are there any other accounts I don't know about?"

"Melanie, I told you I set up that account just to hold the stock money until it could be reinvested. Why would there be other accounts?"

"Why not just put the money in our regular account?"

"Taxes. That money has never been in the US, so there's no US taxes."

"So it's all about tax avoidance?"

"What difference does it make? I'm in jail. Hire the lawyer."

"I'm thinking about it." She hung up.

Franklin wanted to bang the phone receiver against the wall, but he didn't. Melanie was suspicious of him. She probably thought he was leaving and taking the money when the cops got him at the airport, but she wouldn't say it out loud. That wasn't her way. If she admitted to herself that he was leaving, then she'd have to ask herself why, and she didn't want to open that can of worms because then she'd have to examine just what kind of wife she'd been—self-centered, distant, unavailable. Bottom line, she wasn't going to help him at all. He looked up and down the hall, sighed, and dialed Angie's number. It rang almost to voice mail. "Angie?"

"Ronnie, how are you? Had a hard time digging my phone out of my bag. I just finished teaching my morning class."

"I don't know how to tell you this, but I'm in jail."

"I know. I saw on TV."

"I need a lawyer."

"You were leaving without me."

"I was going to send for you. Besides, I wasn't running away. I didn't do anything. I've been under so much pressure, I panicked."

"So Melanie won't help you." She was quiet for a moment. "You're a terrible liar, Ronnie, and I guess I'm the biggest fool in the world. What can I do?"

"I'm going to have to find my own lawyer."

"Yeah, so?"

"I need to use the money in the safe for the retainer."

"You going to tell me the combination? What's to stop me from spending the money?"

"You're not that kind of person. That's one of the things I love about you."

She laughed. "You hope I'm not that kind of person."

"Will you help me?"

"Yeah. I don't know why, but I will."

He told her the combination. "When I get a lawyer, I'll give him your phone number and he'll get in touch about the retainer."

"Okay. So how are you holding up, really?"

"It's not as bad as jail in some movies, but it's bad enough. I'm hoping a lawyer can get this misunderstanding cleared up enough for me to get affordable bail. If I could just get out of here, I could prove I'm innocent."

"I'll be waiting for your call."

"Thanks, Angie. I knew I could count on you."

At 5:30 p.m., Samantha, Joe, and Tess sat together in Joe's Ford Explorer in a metered parking spot in front of Lightning Connections Internet Café on Ninth Street two blocks from Orion College. Joe wore a leather bomber jacket over jeans and a hoody. Tess wore a dark brown wig and fake plastic-frame glasses.

"You two look ridiculous. You're not fooling anyone."

"Smalls knows what we look like. But a stranger's description of the three of us? We'll buy some deniability." Joe looked up and down the street. College-aged people, professor-aged people, business-casual dressed people. "So the cops took Franklin's computer?"

Samantha nodded. "They emptied his office this afternoon."

"What are they going to find?" Joe asked.

"All kinds of incriminating stuff if they know what they're looking for. Programs that were supposedly destroyed in the electrical fire, for starters."

"Could make it look like he did it all," Joe said. "Killed Jackson to cover up the fire."

"All to the good." Tess shoved her hands into her pockets.

"Maybe," Samantha said. "But now, if we take his money, it comes back to this Internet café, instead of his computer."

"It's not a perfect situation," Joe said, "but we'll charge our time on a stolen credit card, move the money to a front company—J & T Cleaners in the Bahamas—as if Franklin were making a purchase, and send you an electronic payment as if it were a consulting fee. Cops can't get any company records, so they can't follow the money. We should be in and out of here in fifteen minutes."

Samantha sighed. "But what about his family? If we take this money, they'll be broke."

"Sam," Tess said, "Ronnie was going to take the money and run. He sold the stock and went to the airport. What do you think he was planning to do to his family?"

"I know; I know. But now he can't do that."

Joe shook his head. "How long do you think he'll stay in jail if he has this money? His family lost that money as soon as he planned to run. Either the lawyers will get it, he'll run with it, or we'll get it. His family isn't in this equation. We need this money and we need him to take the fall. No matter what happens now, his family isn't keeping this money. Okay?"

"Okay."

They got out of the Explorer, fed the meter, went into Lightning Connections, pulled three chairs around a desktop computer in the back, and began going through Franklin's accounts. The local checking had $1,033 in it. The local savings had $500. An Internet bank had $260. The stock account was almost empty as well, though they could see a lot of Leapfrog stock had been sold in the last week. None of those accounts were worth the trouble of stealing from. Then they opened the Cayman Island Bank account. Five dollars. But there had been $562,000 there yesterday.

"That bastard," Joe whispered. "He must have moved the money somewhere else."

"But where?" Tess said. "He didn't trust Angie."

"Look at the times." Samantha pointed out a line of text on the screen. "The money was moved after he was arrested."

Tess put her hand on top of Samantha's. "Maybe the wife found out about the girlfriend."

"Ronnie Franklin," Joe said, "was in over his head the day he was born. There's got to be a way to get that money."

"It's not there," Samantha said. "It's gone. You can see for yourself."

"How do we get a look at the wife's computer?"

"Good luck with all that," Samantha said. "I'm done. I agreed to help you access Ronnie's accounts. The money is gone. Ronnie is in jail. My only chance now is to get Lilypad up and running, so the stock will bounce back up and I'll get a bonus." Samantha cleared the screen and rebooted the machine.

"Fair enough," Joe said. "Let's get out of here."

Outside, the streetlights had turned on. Leroy Smalls was leaning against the Explorer, his dark blue parka zipped up, and his hands thrust into his pockets. Tiny pellets of snow were starting to fall and the wind kicked them around like dust on a baseball diamond. Smalls smiled. "Well, well, all my favorite people. Going to a costume party?"

"What are you doing here, Leroy?" Samantha said.

"Just demonstrating my detection abilities."

"And you've detected that we know one another and we don't care to tell you our business," Joe said.

Smalls looked at Samantha. "You told Meyers that Tess would be back after lunch. He wasn't very happy when he left and hadn't spoken to her. But don't worry; I smoothed it over for you. And you don't have to thank me. We've got plenty of time for you to pay me for watching your back." He turned to Tess. "Did you tell your boy to get my money together? That should be your first priority."

"We're working on it," she said.

"Work faster. I want that money tonight. Think I'm kidding?" He pulled his cell phone out of his pocket. "I've got Gonzalez's twenty-four hour number." He stuck the phone in

Joe's chest. "I'm losing patience with you. You're not screwing me over. You are going to pay to play. Nine p.m. tonight at Jimmy's Deli."

"Where's it at?"

"Look it up, smart ass." Smalls walked away.

Joe, Tess, and Samantha got into the Explorer. "Why didn't you tell me?" Samantha said.

"Relax," Joe said. "We were going to pay him out of our end. There was no reason to involve you."

"But now there isn't any money to pay him with."

"Let me think," Joe said.

"At least start the car and get the heat going," Tess said.

Joe started the SUV.

"How much does he want?" Samantha asked.

"Ten thousand."

"I can't get that out of petty cash. I gave you fifty thousand to begin with. Can't you take it out of that?"

Tess gripped Joe's arm. She didn't want to kill Samantha to cover their tracks. "Is it plan B or plan C? Because I'm still troubled by plan C."

"Don't worry," Joe said. "Let me think." He turned in the driver's seat so that he could look at Tess in the front and Samantha in the back at the same time. "Now, Smalls is, essentially, blackmailing us with our own fear. We pay him or he directs the police to us and the police find out we're dirty. Which means—"

Tess cut in, "He doesn't know anything. He just has suspicions."

Joe continued. "But we can't call his bluff and ride it out because the cops might actually find some evidence."

"I told you," Samantha said, "if they've got half a brain, they'll have plenty of evidence when they're finished with Ronnie's computer. Even if computer forensics can't pull anything off the melted hard drive."

"But none of that points to you or us."

Samantha thought for a moment. "That's right. So what?"

"What if you call the cops and tell them that Smalls is blackmailing you?"

"What? Are you crazy? I don't want the cops looking at me."

"They're already looking at you. They're looking at everyone at Leapfrog. Tell them that Smalls is going to claim you were in with Ronnie on a scheme that led to Jackson being killed. Tell them it's a lie, but that a rumor like that, on top of the product delay and Jackson's death, would be the final straw that would break the company. That you'd lose your job and your retirement. That's what Smalls is holding over you."

"They arrest Leroy and he's off our backs." Samantha nodded. "It might work."

"Might work?" Tess said. "It's genius. Even if Smalls wriggles out of the blackmail charge, he'll still be discredited."

"So he won't be able to shake you down in the future," Joe said.

"I don't know if I can do this," Samantha said.

"I understand," Joe said. "You're afraid the cops will catch you in a lie. But you're not lying. You keep it simple. You call the cops. You've already met these cops; you know them. You tell them you're supposed to deliver the money. Tonight. Nine p.m. at Jimmy's Deli. Tess'll walk you through it. She'll be by your side every step of the way. I'd do it, but if the cops find out about me, that raises too many questions."

"Tess will be with me?"

"I'll be holding your hand," Tess said.

"But you stood up the cops."

"I'll be fine. It'll take some of the focus off you."

Joe looked at Samantha expectantly. "You got the cop's business card?"

Samantha dug around in her handbag. "Right here."

"Call him up," Tess said.

Meyers and Gonzalez sat side by side in their overcoats on the cream-colored sofa in the Franklins' living room, drinking coffee from china cups. Melanie Franklin sat opposite them in a matching overstuffed chair, her legs tucked under her. She wore dark blue stretch pants and a pink V-neck pullover. A single strand of large fake pearls hung around her neck. The coffee service sat on a bamboo tray on the coffee table between them and a fire burned in the gas fireplace at the end of the room.

153

Gonzalez leaned forward and set his coffee cup on the table. "Sorry to bother you during dinner time, Mrs. Franklin."

"It's no trouble. My daughter won't be home for another hour. More coffee?"

"I'm fine. As I said on the phone, we want to ask you a few questions about your husband's movements. You have the right to have an attorney present."

She waved off his remark. "I'm happy to help if I can."

Gonzalez took a small audio recorder out of his pocket and set it on the coffee table. He turned it on. "This is Detective Gonzalez. I'm interviewing Melanie Franklin. Also present is Detective Meyers. Mrs. Franklin, your husband, Ronnie Franklin, sustained a number of injuries earlier this week. What day did those injuries occur?"

"Tuesday."

"Did he fall down the stairs?"

She looked from Gonzalez to Meyers and back. "Is that what he said? He told me he was mugged leaving work, but I didn't believe him."

Meyers cut in. "Why not?"

"He said he had a call from work—it was eight p.m. or so. I—" Melanie dabbed her eyes with a tissue. "I'm sorry, this is all unsettling."

"Take your time," Gonzalez said.

"I was afraid he had a girlfriend . . ."

"Why?"

"Just a feeling, you know, some things just didn't seem right. Anyway, I followed him to Ridgeview Apartments. I saw him meet a woman and go into her apartment. I was devastated. You know, I was assuming the worst. I came home. I couldn't sleep. I was wandering around the house. Later, eleven p.m. or so, I heard him come in. I came downstairs to confront him. He was all beat up. It scared me. I wanted him to go to the emergency room, but he wouldn't go. He claimed it happened leaving the office. But I knew he hadn't been to the office. So then I wasn't sure. Was he having an affair or was he mixed up in something crazy?" She shrugged.

"What did the woman look like?"

"I don't really know, other than she was blonde. She was all bundled up and it was dark in the parking lot."

"And you watched him go into her apartment?"

She nodded. "I wrote down the address."

Gonzalez's phone rang. "Just a minute. I'm stopping the recording." He turned off the audio recorder and answered the phone. "Hello?"

"Detective Gonzalez? This is Samantha Bartel." She told him about the blackmail threat.

"Really?" Gonzalez glanced at Meyers. "Meet us at the police station." He hung up and turned the audio recorder back on.

He smiled at Melanie Franklin. "Restarting the recording. Sorry about that. We're continuing the interview with Mrs. Franklin. Did your husband ever explain what happened?"

"No, he wouldn't tell me a thing. Then on Thursday you arrested him at the airport."

"Did you know he was leaving town?"

"No."

Meyers watched Melanie worrying her hands. "You're angry with your husband, aren't you?"

"Yes. Yes, I am."

"But you don't think your husband killed Stuart Jackson, do you?"

"Ronnie couldn't kill anyone."

Gonzalez turned off the recorder. "Could you give us that woman's address?"

"Sure. Let me get it out of my car."

Melanie came back with a scrap of paper that had Angie's apartment number scrawled on it and rewrote the address onto a note card and handed it to Gonzalez.

"Thanks. Please don't make contact with this woman. We'd like to be the first ones to talk with her."

Gonzalez and Meyers walked down the Franklins' driveway to their unmarked Impala parked on the street. The night was so quiet they could hear the snow squeak under their shoes. "What do you think?" Meyers asked.

"I think Mrs. Franklin is hoping her husband is just an adulterer, but she doesn't quite believe it."

"The address the same as the one Franklin gave us for the girlfriend?"

"I think so."

Meyers nodded. "Who was on the phone?"

"Samantha Bartel. She claims Leroy Smalls is blackmailing her."

Meyers was incredulous. "Smalls? Hard to believe."

"That's what I would have said before he held back the parking deck video. Now I don't know."

They got into their car, Gonzalez behind the wheel, and pulled away from the curb. Gonzalez filled in Meyers about Samantha's accusation.

Meyers shook his head. "The whole time Leroy was on the job I never heard anything crooked about him."

"Look, it's easy to settle. We just wire her up and let her go to the deli. If he's a bum, we've got him. And if not, Ms. Bartel has a lot of explaining to do." Gonzalez stopped at a stop sign and put on his left turn signal. "They all work at Leapfrog Technologies. Who knows? Maybe this will help loosen up the Jackson case. Help us find out Franklin's motivation."

"And Tess Campbell is coming with her?" Meyers asked.

Gonzalez made his turn. "Yeah. That's what she says."

"Wonder where she ran off to today?"

Samantha and Tess were waiting in the lobby of the police station when Gonzalez and Meyers arrived. The police station lobby was 1960s institutional: beige painted walls and a row of light green fiberglass chairs lined up under a picture window that was directly opposite the scuffed-up Formica-topped Sergeant's counter.

"Ladies," Gonzalez said. He opened the door in the half wall extending from the counter and ushered them through. Samantha hobbled along on her crutches, taking care not to bang her leg cast into any furniture, Tess trailing close behind her. They took the elevator to the second-floor hall and pushed through the glass doors to the squad room, where Meyers had pulled a few extra chairs up to Gonzalez's desk.

"Ms. Bartel, Ms. Campbell, please sit down," Meyers said. "Can I get you some coffee?"

Samantha and Tess shook their heads. Gonzalez sat opposite them. Meyers sat on the corner of the gray metal desk across the aisle. "Okay," Gonzalez said, "so you claim Leroy Smalls is blackmailing you."

"It's more than a claim. I couldn't believe it when he came to me today demanding money," Samantha said.

"Ma'am," Meyers said, "you got to admit that it sounds far-fetched."

"It's the truth."

Gonzalez continued. "So he said?"

"Ten thousand dollars or he'd tell you I'm involved in some sort of conspiracy to defraud Leapfrog that led to Stuart's murder."

"But you're not involved?

Samantha threw her hands up. "What conspiracy? You have access to everything at the office. On top of the fire and the murder, an accusation like that could ruin the company. I'm fifty-four years old. I can't start over."

"What about you, Ms. Campbell? You involved in a con-spiracy to defraud Leapfrog Technologies?"

"No. That's crazy talk."

Meyers cut in. "Where were you this afternoon?"

"I had class and a presentation. By the time I got back to Leapfrog, you were gone."

"Really?"

"Check with the college."

"Why didn't you call us? You knew we were looking for you."

"Okay. I apologize. I dropped the ball. I guess I didn't think it was that big a deal since I'm only an intern."

"We still want to interview you."

"Sure. How about Monday morning?"

Meyers nodded.

Gonzalez continued. "So why are you here now?"

Tess glanced at Samantha and squeezed her hand. "I'm just here as moral support."

Meyers looked from Tess to Samantha. "So you two are old friends?"

"We just met a week ago," Tess said. "But sometimes you meet someone and everything just clicks."

Gonzalez and Meyers shared a glance. Then Gonzalez pushed his hands together. "Okay. So Smalls wants the money tonight?"

"Yeah," Samantha said. "We're supposed to take it to Jimmy's Deli at nine p.m."

"Do you have the money?"

"No."

"So that's why you've come to us."

Samantha shook her head. "I wouldn't give him the money even if I had it. I haven't done anything, and it would just make me look guilty."

"Would you wear a wire?"

She gave Gonzalez a hard look. "Smalls is a big guy. And he carries a gun."

"The wire is the only way to get him off your back."

"You guys will be right there?"

Gonzalez nodded. "Without a doubt."

Samantha glanced at Tess. Tess nodded. "Okay then," Samantha said, "but only if you're really there."

Meyers turned to Gonzalez. "We could use the marked bills in evidence from that drug buy."

"I'll call the Captain. Go sign out three thousand. Take Owen with you. From here on out, we want plenty of witnesses."

Samantha and Tess came through the front door of Jimmy's Italian Deli just at 9:00 p.m. They stood at the hostess's station for a moment, letting their eyes adjust to the light. Jimmy's Italian Deli was a family friendly pizza parlor with plastic, red-check tablecloths over square tables, dark-stained booths down the walls, and a salad bar covered by a prominent sneeze guard located in the middle of the room. In the back, a big screen TV was tuned to a sports network. Leroy Smalls sat at a table with a good view of the TV. The only waitress left in the deli, a young, dark-haired woman wearing a loose pony-tail and a tomato-sauce splattered white apron, came up to the hostess's station. "I'm sorry; we're done serving."

"That's okay," Samantha said. She waved at Smalls. "We're just meeting someone."

Samantha and Tess made their way back to Smalls's table. He smiled. "Have a seat, ladies. The second game is about to start. Would you like a beer or anything?"

"I'm fine," Samantha said. She sat across from Smalls with her cast out in the aisle and leaned her crutches against a nearby table.

"Me, too," Tess said. She sat to Samantha's left, so she had a clear view of the front door.

"Got my package?" Smalls asked.

"That's what we wanted to talk about," Tess said. "Ten thousand was too much to gather up on such short notice. We've got three thousand here; we can get the rest by Monday."

Smalls rose up in his seat. "You think you can play with me?"

Samantha raised her hands in surrender. "Just give us a chance. We don't want any trouble."

Smalls sat back down and sipped his rum and coke. "Give me the three thousand. On Monday you'll give me ten thousand. Before noon."

"Ten thousand? We only owe seven more."

"Ten thousand. Or do you want me to go to my old buddies Gonzalez and Meyers and tell them all about your involvement with Ronnie."

"What involvement?" Samantha asked.

"Don't act stupid. You screw with me, and you'll have them squeezing you for money as well."

Samantha slid a fat envelope containing $3,000 in marked one hundred dollar bills across the red-checked tablecloth. Smalls glanced inside the envelope and put it into the inside pocket of his navy sports coat. "Thank you, ladies. I knew you'd eventually see things my way."

"So we're done here?" Samantha asked.

"Monday," Smalls said. "Before noon."

Samantha hobbled out of the deli, Tess close behind her. An old neon sign flashed "Jimmy's Italian Deli" over their heads in green and red. Gonzalez and Meyers were waiting on the sidewalk, their hands in their pockets. "Good job, Ms. Bartel,"

Meyers said. "We've got you recorded, so we can take your statement tomorrow."

"He's got the marked bills?" Gonzalez asked.

"Inside pocket of his blazer," Samantha replied.

"Do you need a ride?" Meyers asked.

"No, we're fine." She took the microphone out of her coat pocket. "I'll let you have this back, though."

"Thanks," Meyers said. "Until tomorrow. Give me a call when you're up and about."

"Let's get this done," Gonzalez said. Gonzalez and Meyers went into the deli.

Samantha let out a sigh and leaned down into her crutches. She felt exhausted and alone. Her entire future depended on what happened between Smalls and the detectives. She wanted to believe she was safe, but it seemed too good to be true. Tess walked into the street as if she were hailing a cab and looked up the hill at the cars parked along the curb. A blue Ford Explorer flashed its headlights, pulled out of its parking spot, and rolled down toward them. Joe was behind the wheel. Samantha and Tess got in when he pulled up in front of them. "Everything's set," Tess said.

Joe nodded. "I figured as much." He looked in the back seat at Samantha. "Where to?"

She sat back in her seat and fastened her seatbelt. "Drop me off at Leapfrog. My car is in the deck."

They rode in silence. Joe pulled up to the curb at the bottom of the parking deck. It was well lit and there was no one in sight. "Where's your car?"

"I'll be okay. The elevator's right there." Samantha opened her door to get out.

"Good luck," Tess said.

"You won't see us again," Joe added.

"What do I do about the cops?"

"They have you recorded. Stick with your story. Everything will be fine."

"How can you be so sure?"

"The cops have Smalls and the cops have Franklin. They're on a one-way street to closing the case; they're not turning around."

Samantha shut the door on the Explorer and hobbled away.

Joe pulled back into traffic. "So," Tess said, "what's next?"

"Jonny's boys won't be looking for us until tomorrow. Let's see if we can get a look at the computers at Franklin's house."

Joe and Tess drove to Clareview Heights, where they sat in the Explorer half a block down the street from the Franklins' house. It was 10:30 p.m. The night sky was overcast. The street was quiet except for a cluster of cars parked at the curb in front of a neighbor's house, where light and party sounds spilled out to the street. They'd watched the Franklins' daughter drive away in an old blue Toyota van. They assumed Franklin's wife was in the house, but they were tired of waiting. "Give her a call," Joe said.

Tess called the Franklins' home phone. No one answered. The phone rang until it rolled over to voice mail. Tess hung up and tried again. Same thing. They walked down the sidewalk and up the driveway to the Franklins' front door, the snow crunching under their feet. When they tripped the motion sensor on the outdoor lights, the lights switched on, illuminating the limestone steps and the stained glass front door. Joe rang the bell. No one answered. He rang the bell again. No answer. Tess picked the lock and opened the door. "Hello," she called out. "Hello."

They shut the door, took off their winter gloves and put on latex gloves. They did a quick walk-through of the downstairs. No one. The lights were on in the kitchen and in the stairwell to the upstairs. A desktop computer sat on a built-in desk in the kitchen. They went upstairs. The hallway light was on. They could hear a murmuring of voices. Tess pushed open the door to the master bedroom. A woman she assumed was Mrs. Franklin lay on the bed on top of the covers dressed in a pink-striped fleece robe and sheepskin slippers. Her eyes were closed. Tess slipped into the room. The TV was tuned to a home decorating show.

On the night table closest to Mrs. Franklin, Tess saw an empty wine glass and a half-full prescription pill bottle. Tess tiptoed up to the bed and picked up the bottle. Sleeping pills. She put a finger to Mrs. Franklin's throat to check for a pulse

161

and then lay her hand gently on the upper part of Mrs. Franklin's chest. She smiled to herself, turned to leave, stopped, removed Mrs. Franklin's slippers, and pulled the bedspread over her. In the hallway, Joe was waiting for her. They went back down to the computer in the kitchen. "The missus is knocked out on wine and sleeping pills. Her breathing and pulse are fine. I don't think a tornado could wake her."

Joe pulled in an extra chair from the dining room, and they both sat down in front of the computer. A post-it note stuck to the corner of the monitor had the computer password on it. The passwords for the financial accounts were all saved on the computer. All the accounts were the same as the ones they'd checked at Lightning Connections. Joe looked at Tess. "We just can't catch a break."

They went through the house room by room, dumping drawers, looking for any account information that would tell them where the Leapfrog Technologies stock money had gone, but they didn't find anything. All they found for their trouble was $215, four credit cards and some modest jewelry, all of which they left in place. "This is worse than when we hit the girlfriend's place," Tess said.

Joe started to speak, but they heard the garage door lifting. They ran to the front windows. The outside lights had turned on. The daughter was pulling into the driveway with two other girls in her blue van. Once her van disappeared into the garage, Joe opened the front door and he and Tess stepped out onto the front stoop and stood there. They could hear hip-hop music blasting from the daughter's van in the garage. The music stopped. Doors slammed. Girl voices. The garage door started lowering. Joe and Tess scurried down the sidewalk to the street just as the garage door came in contact with the garage floor. A few minutes later, they were sitting in the Explorer, at the curb, a half block from the house they'd broken into, laughing.

Joe put the Explorer into drive and pulled away. "I'd love to see the look on their faces right now."

"Drawers out everywhere. Momma Franklin completely out of it."

"Did you catch the time when they walked in?"

"What?"

162

"Just want to time off the police response."

The police were racing into Clareview Heights with lights and sirens just as Joe and Tess were making a right turn out of the subdivision. "There's some important taxpayers in that neighborhood."

"It's time to get out of town."

"First we have to look in the girlfriend's safe."

"You think there's still anything in there?"

"I'm not going to leave forty thousand on the table."

They crossed town to the Ridgeview apartments. The lights were off in Angie's apartment and her car was gone. Joe rang the doorbell. No one answered. Tess picked the lock. They walked back through the dark apartment. Joe turned on the light in the closet. There was a knock at the front door. They ignored it. The knocking turned into pounding. "Open the door. I know you're in there."

Tess went to the door in the dark and looked out the peephole. A bearded man in a blue parka stood on the front steps. Tess opened the door with the chain on. "Get away from here or I'm calling the cops."

"You're not Angie. Who are you?"

She could smell alcohol on his breath. "You're at the wrong apartment. Go away."

"This is Angie's apartment."

"This is my apartment. I don't know any Angie. I'm calling the cops."

She shut the door and locked it. She looked out the peephole. The man stood there a moment, acting befuddled, and then left. Tess went to the window and watched until the man got in a car parked in the visitors' parking and drove away. Joe joined her in the living room. "Thirty-five thousand and change. Who was that?"

"Extra boyfriend. Already drunk."

"Is he gone?"

"Drove away."

"Let's get out of here."

Joe shut the door behind them. As they were walking down the sidewalk toward their Explorer, an outdoor light came on, illuminating the front door of an interior apartment on the next apartment block. The woman with the little dog came out; the woman bundled up in her heavy down coat, the dog in a little green and red plaid dog coat. They passed one another on the sidewalk, Joe walking single-file behind Tess to make room. "Hi, again," the woman said.

"Hi," Tess said.

"Are you new here?"

"We have friends on the next block."

"The visitor parking up around the other side would probably be closer."

"Thanks."

Joe and Tess walked into the parking lot. Joe looked over his shoulder at the woman. She was standing with her dog by the light pole. "Very observant."

"Woman by herself at night both times," Tess said.

They waited until the woman with the little dog turned the corner before they got into their Explorer. "I'm cold," Tess said.

Joe started the SUV and turned the heat on high. Cold air blew out of the ducts. "Give it a minute." They drove out of the parking lot and headed back across town to their apartment. "What's left?"

"We're all packed," Tess said. "What do you want to do about my car?"

"We'll park it downtown near that seedy strip club and leave the keys in it."

11: New Starts

Monday morning at 8:50 a.m., Angie was rushing around her apartment looking for her car keys. She was supposed to lead a yoga class at the country club at 9:00 a.m. The keys weren't in her handbag. They weren't in her coat pockets. They weren't in the ceramic tray on the table by the door. They weren't on the coffee table. She finally found them next to her coffee cup on the bathroom sink counter. She slipped on her sheepskin-lined boots, pulled on her parka, checked the pockets for her black leather gloves, and started toward the door when the doorbell rang.

A bald man with a tanned face and bushy blond eyebrows stood at her door. "Ms. Delcor?" He smiled reassuringly. "I'm Wally Smits. We talked on the phone."

"Oh, yeah," Angie said, "I forgot all about you. Come in. I'm in a hurry. I'm almost late for work. Be right back." She rushed into her bedroom, turned on the light in the closet, dug the safe combination out of her handbag, and opened the safe. All she found was the notebook that listed the dates and amounts of Franklin's deposits. She got down on her knees and felt around inside. Nothing but the steel walls. She looked at her watch. 8:55. There was nothing here. Nothing. She went back into the living room. She still had the notebook in her hand. "Mr. Smits?"

"Something wrong?"

"The money's not in the safe. I don't know what to say. I have to leave right now or I'll be late for work. Can I call you later?"

"It would be easier—"

"I'm going to be late for work." She guided him out the door in front of her and locked the door behind herself. "I'll call in an hour."

She left Smits standing on the sidewalk watching her as she rushed toward her car. Where could the money be? Ronnie was going to think she took it. But was the money even there? Had Ronnie already taken it? Breathe. Breathe. There was nothing she could do right now except teach her class. She'd have two hours free afterward to figure this out. Maybe the money was in a bag on the floor. She'd tear that closet apart. If the money were there, she'd find it. She drove across Ridgeview Avenue and into the Cloverdale Golf and Country Club parking lot. Good thing she lived across the street. She couldn't afford to lose her job. Particularly with Ronnie in jail.

Samantha sat at the head of the table in the fifth floor conference room at Leapfrog Technologies, leading a meeting with the Lilypad design team. She was wearing her brown skirt suit. Her laptop sat open on the table in front of her. The design team, four men and two women still dressed like college students in faded jeans and old sweaters, sat around the table looking at their open laptops and Samantha at the same time. "Has everyone seen the new code Allison and Bob developed over the weekend?"

Allison, a tall woman with close-cropped red hair, and Bob, an unshaven man wearing a black knit cap, bumped fists across the table. The four other programmers sitting around the table nodded. "We're going to use it as the basis for a fresh approach to the third phase. Let's see what we can come up with by the end of the day." The programmers picked up their laptops and left the room. Samantha sat for a moment studying the new code. Hard to believe no one had developed this the first time around, but it made sense.

Detective Meyers stuck his head in the door. "Ms. Bartel, how are you?"

"I'm fine, thank you. What can I do for you?" She gestured toward the chair nearest hers. "Have a seat. Did you need more info from me about Smalls? I thought we covered everything on Saturday."

166

Meyers kept on standing in the doorway. "No, your statement is complete. I'm looking for Ms. Campbell."

Samantha shrugged. "I don't know. Friday was the last day of her internship. Have you called her cell or tried her house?"

"I haven't been able to get a hold of her. I thought perhaps since you're such good friends—"

Samantha shook her head and shrugged. "Sorry."

Meyers disappeared into the hall. Samantha pushed the printouts into a stack, hopped up on her good leg, and reached for her crutches. Joe and Tess had been exactly right. She was completely in the clear. Leroy and Ronnie were both discredited. No one would believe a word they said. It was their own fault. All she had to do was stick to her story. She had her job. She was in the good graces of the board of directors. And now Lilypad was almost in the bag. She hobbled out into the hall. There was every chance that the next few years were going to be very good to her. Maybe now she'd be able to focus on finding a mate.

Meyers drove over to the Green Valley Apartments and found Tess Campbell's apartment. No one was parked in the assigned parking spot. He got out of his car without bothering to put his parka on. The wind was cold. He tucked his chin down and hunched his shoulders down in his blue blazer. The snow on the sidewalk had been trampled into icy footprints, but the sun was hot enough to melt the edges of the ice pack. He knocked on her door. No answer. He knocked louder. No one. He turned the doorknob. The door opened. "Ms. Campbell."

He went inside. "Ms. Campbell." The furniture was there, and the refrigerator had lettuce, cold cuts, milk, and beer in it, but the bedroom closet and the bathroom cabinets were empty. He sat down on the living room sofa and called Gonzalez. "Marty, Campbell is gone. I'm in her apartment. Looks like she left in a hurry. Everything's here but her clothes and toiletries. Have we got her car license plate numbers?"

"Is it worth the trouble?"

"Dotting I's and crossing T's."

"I'll check the DMV," Gonzalez said.

Meyers put his phone back into his pocket. Maybe she just went away for the weekend. He stood up and scanned the room. There was nothing except the furniture and the TV — no pictures, no knick-knacks, no personal items of any kind. Who was Tess Campbell? The furniture came with the apartment. He needed to see the apartment lease. He got his phone back out and called the Green Valley Apartments management company.

Joe and Tess were driving down the salt-stained interstate in the blue Ford Explorer. The countryside was leafless and brown, with a scattering of snow puddles. At this pace, by evening they'd be out of snow country and the grass would be starting to green. Joe was wearing khaki pants with a red checked shirt and a blue cardigan sweater. He'd shaved off his mustache and darkened the gray in his hair. Tess was wearing skinny jeans with a turquoise boat-neck sweater. Her hair was dyed auburn. "Eighty-five thousand."

"Minus expenses," Joe said.

"Minus expenses. Would have been ninety and a lot less trouble if we'd emptied the girlfriend's safe the first time."

"It was a calculated risk. If we hadn't tried, we'd still be wondering. Just came up short."

"You know we stepped over the line back there."

"Over the line?"

"With the wife. Going after the money at her house. She was a civilian."

"I don't think so," he said. "The money was fair game as long as Franklin had a chance of getting it back. Those were joint accounts. He could have wasted that money paying lawyer fees. But the money wasn't there. So Franklin couldn't get it. The wife saved herself."

"We got to do better."

"All's well that ends well." Billboards indicated that a town was coming up. "Hey, where do you want to eat lunch?"

"It's a little early."

"I think this is the last decent stop for sixty miles."

"Let's sit down in a restaurant. I'd like a real salad."

"Okay. It would be good to get out of the truck for a bit."

"How long is it going to take to get to Miami?"

"Tomorrow sometime. Depends on where we stop to switch cars."

"Two months off. Lying on the beach, eating in good restaurants, going out to clubs. Heaven on earth."

He patted her leg. "You deserve it."

She smiled softly. "Say, you think Franklin really killed Jackson? Nobody thought he was capable of it."

"Does it matter? Maybe he didn't do it. But he's still probably going to jail. Anyway, it was a dead end for us. I hope his wife enjoys her money." He read the exit sign. "I think this is our turnoff." He started down the exit ramp.

"What will we do after Miami?"

"I don't know," he said. "I'm sure something will turn up. I'm not going to worry about it now."

He pulled up to the stop sign at the end of the ramp and looked to his left. There were no cars in sight. He turned right onto the two-lane blacktop road. A cluster of gas stations was in sight. "Hey, honey, why don't you pull out your laptop and find us a restaurant?"

A Note From the Author

Thanks for reading *The Computer Heist*. Please consider telling your friends or posting a short review on a review site of your choice. Your review will help other readers choose books that they'll enjoy.

I'd love to hear from you. You can reach me at my website: michaelpking.org.

The Computer Heist is the second novel of the Travelers series. The third novel, *The Blackmail Photos*, will be available in the fall of 2016.

The Travelers
The Traveling Man: Book One
The Computer Heist: Book Two
The Blackmail Photos: Book Three

Made in United States
Orlando, FL
13 May 2024